THE CASE
— of the —
GHOST *of*
CHRISTMAS
MORNING

The Second *Anty Boisjoly* Mystery

THE CASE — of the — GHOST of CHRISTMAS MORNING

1	The Final Flight of Flaps Fleming	1
2	The Intrepid Interception of the Inevitable Inspector	12
3	The Subtle Sign at the Scene of the Crime	22
4	The Affair of the Phantom Farewell	32
5	The Mysterious Meeting in the Manger at Midnight	44
6	The Candid Revelations of the Christmas Celebrations	61
7	The Strange Scene on Saint Stephen's Steeple Seen	74
8	Hildy Discovers Her Hidden Depths	89
9	Zero Zone at the Zeppelin's Zenith	101
10	The Curious Comportment of the Common Cuckoo	119
11	Sainted Stephen's Sticky End	130
12	The Debutante Aunt's Debut	142
13	Whither Wanes the Weather Vanes	155
14	The Vanishing Visitor of the Solicitous Solicitor	170
15	Devious Dealings Over Dunkirk	183
16	Tense Dark Work in a Dense Dark Wood	193
17	Six Sinister Secrets	201
18	Astray and Adrift in a Drift	217
19	The Seriously Circuitous Solution	227
20	The Twist in the Case of the Ghost of Christmas Morning	207
	Anty Boisjoly Mysteries	252

CHAPTER ONE

The Final Flight
of Flaps Fleming

"MERRY CHRISTMAS ANTY DEAR. There's a dead body under the tree."

...was very nearly the last thing I expected to hear upon arrival at my Aunty Boisjoly's cosy, sixteen-bedroom burrow in snowy Hertfordshire. She was the shy aunty, you see, and not usually very clever at gift-giving. I still haven't grown into the spats she gave me for my christening.

But I had rather owed Aunty Azalea Boisjoly a visit since the untimely passing of her brother and my father — not coincidentally one and the same chap — left us both similarly alone against the fates. So here I was, in the delightful dairy town of Graze Hill, tracking Aunty Azalea to the warm and well-appointed Victorian-style drawing-room of her country seat, Herding House.

"A body, Aunty?" I said. "I don't even see a tree. I'm not disappointed, mind you, in either case. I mention it more as a point of order."

"We don't have a tree, Anty," said Aunty. "I can't bear to have strangers in the house, you know that. Instead, there's a glass bauble on the rubber plant in the library. Would you like to see it?"

"In good time," I said. "First, if there isn't one in the house, to what tree do you refer and, perhaps more pressingly, to what body?"

Aunty Azalea was always the eccentric one in a family not widely famed for an extravagant excess of marbles. She was very like my father and myself physically — tall and narrow with a pasty-white and chestnut livery and the famous Boisjoly eyebrows that give the impression that we're easily and constantly surprised — but in addition to belonging to the school that pronounced the family name "Bo-juhlay", like the wine region, as opposed to "Boo-juhlay", like the wine region, she was timid almost to the degree of genius. She was to bashfulness what that Pythagoras chap was to sorting out the area of the square of the hypotenuse once and for all.

"Flaps Fleming is dead," said Aunty Azalea.

"I'm very sorry to hear that," I said, glancing about for, I suppose, context. "Was he, you know, an actual chap, this Flaps Fleming, or a beloved goose or some such?"

"He was my neighbour, Anty. Major Aaron Fleming."

"Quite sure?" I asked. "It would make a good name for a goose, Flaps."

"I was hoping you'd know what to do."

"Of course, Aunty dear, leave it all to me," I said. "Are we quite certain, though, that there's anything to be done? If the poor chap's already snuffed it then I'd have to say that the situation's largely out of our hands."

"I mean about the police and all that." Aunty Azalea fidgeted nervously with a heavy, velvet curtain as a pretext for hiding herself in it. "The major has been murdered."

"Murdered? Are you quite sure?"

"He's under a Christmas tree in his living room with a knife in his back."

"I see," I said. "I think I'm twigging to the state of affairs now, Aunty, but your telling was something of a slow burn, if you don't mind me saying so. You'll probably want to jump straight to the punchline, in future, when recounting the discovery of a murder."

"I'll bear it in mind," said Aunty, munificently.

"Sound policy, favourite aunt. Doubtless my late father mentioned my modest reputation among London's smart set as a problem-solver."

"I don't think so," said Aunty, meditatively. "He only mentioned that you were a highly effective spendthrift."

"That is, I confess, my principal occupation," I confirmed, "and it consumes most of my waking hours, but I have my fingers in many pies, running the gamut from clubbing, idling, and man-about-towning, to helping mates through scrapes. Perhaps you heard of the twin tragedies that befell the Canterfell family this past summer?"

"No."

"No? It was in all the papers. They made Fiddles Canterfell an earl, in the end, rather than hanging him for murder, thanks in no small part to me. How about the Fernsby-Loftis affair at the Ritz last year?"

Aunty peered at me from behind the curtain, like a nervous chorus girl. "I don't believe so. Who died?"

"Well, nobody, in the literal sense, it was more in the line of an ill-advised wedding toast. But I was able to convince the bride's father that, in the rich architectural tradition of the Loftis family, a gargoyle is regarded as a thing of great beauty."

"I don't know that it's pertinent to the situation at hand, Anty," said Aunt Azalea uncertainly. "What did they do when they found your father?"

"Scraped him off the tracks with putty knives, I'm told," I said. "But that doesn't apply here. What you want is to involve the local constabulary, straight away."

"But it's Christmas day."

"There is that," I agreed, "but in my experience the forces of law and order like to be kept abreast of this sort of thing, irrespective of the season."

"I'm so glad you're here, Anty," said Aunty, folding herself yet deeper into the rich purple drapery. "I couldn't bear to be questioned by the police."

"I regret, Aunty, that may prove unavoidable, but I'll do what I can to spare you human interaction. Is that the bell?" I referred to the leather pull next to the fireplace. I gave it a jingle and entertained myself with the whisky decanter and soda syphon until Puckeridge, Aunty's longtime butler and head of household staff, appeared at the drawing-room door. I'd never met the man before arriving at the manor that day, but I'd understood from my father that Puckeridge was local talent, the second son of a proud dairy family, and he'd acquired the equivalent of a PhD in butlering at some of the great houses of Bedfordshire. He was accordingly as correct as high tea and otherwise a stout representative of his beef and milk-fed heritage, generous of jowl and midships.

"Were you able to locate Miss Boisjoly, sir?"

"I did, thanks very much, Puckeridge. She was just where

you guessed she'd be, in the drawing-room. Still is, in fact, wrapped in that curtain."

"I'm pleased to have been of service."

"In that case, Puckeridge, I have some jolly good news for you. We need someone to pop into town and fetch the constable."

"Very good, sir."

"You'll probably want to know why," I ventured.

"If you deem it necessary, sir."

"Seems your neighbour's been carved for Christmas," I said. "Do you know this Flaps Fleming chap?"

"Major Aaron Fleming is our neighbour, sir," said Puckeridge with a nod so subtle it might have been telepathic. "He lives in the cottage on the hill."

"Point of order, Puckeridge," I said. "He used to live on the cottage on the hill, which is the gist of that which we need you to confide to the constable. Graze Hill does have a constable, does it not?"

"It does, sir. We share a police station with the town of Steeple Herding, where your train arrived this morning."

"Excellent," I said. "I'd send Vickers, you understand, but, well, you understand." I referred, of course, to my own valet, who had accompanied me to Graze Hill. Vickers had been my father's valet and his father's before him, and his age was the subject of much conjecture.

"Of course, Mister Boisjoly," said Puckeridge. "Mister Vickers is currently resting on some linen in the below-stairs laundry. I've taken the liberty of unpacking your bags in the Heath Room."

"Heath Room?"

"First floor, second left, sir. Overlooking the pastures and, as a point of uncommon interest, the cottage of Major Fleming."

"Was major his active rank, Puckeridge?"

"It is an honorific, sir," said Puckeridge. "Major Fleming was a hero of the Great War."

"That was a decade ago," I said. "Should I have heard of him? Was he one of those iron-willed blighters who took and held some strategically indispensable bit of no-man's land with just a riding crop and a bucket of British pluck?"

"He was a flying ace, to my understanding."

"Ah, a flyboy.

"In the vernacular of the time, yes sir. He flew several hundred sorties over France and Belgium, I understand, and is credited with shooting down forty-one enemy aircraft."

"Is that impressive?" I asked. "Forty-one isn't much of a score in darts, and the skillset strikes me as similar."

"Five air combat victories is the customary requirement for achieving the status of ace, I believe."

"Ah, well, different game, different rules. Did the major live alone in the cottage?"

"He did, sir."

"Had he lived there long?"

"The Flemings have been a part of Graze Hill and the area for generations," said Puckeridge, with the fluent authority of the butler with local knowledge. "The major took occupancy of Tannery Lodge, one of the family dwellings, at the end of the war."

"My aunt says that she saw him this morning, or at any

rate she saw his earthly remains. Were you aware of that?"

"I was not acquainted with Miss Boisjoly's movements until just now, sir."

"It might become necessary for someone to confirm where she was and when."

"That may prove difficult, sir," said Puckeridge with a vague eyebrow of resentment cocked toward the cocoon of drapery which enveloped my aunt. "Miss Boisjoly is often quite circumspect with the household staff."

"Do you hear that Aunty?" I called. "The staff have noticed that you hide in the curtains."

"I'm not hiding in the curtains," came the muffled reply. "I'm examining them... for moths. You know how I feel about moths."

"Miss Boisjoly is very vigilant with regards to the moth problem," confirmed Puckeridge.

"I'll just bet she is," I said. "Thank you, Puckeridge. You'd best be conveying our warmest compliments of the season to the local constabulary."

I left Aunty Azalea to her study of the British moth and imitation thereof and retired to the Heath Room. Vickers and I had arrived at Steeple Herding only an hour ago on the Christmas morning omnibus which, in the spirit of the season, had stopped to pay its respects to stations it hadn't seen in years, and often lingered to catch up on old times. I was looking forward to the comatose quiet that is English dairy country in the wintertime. I was, if it's not introducing the nuts before the soup, soon to be disappointed.

As advertised, my room looked out onto the eponymous heath, and it was magnificent. At the absolute worst of times

Hertfordshire farmland is a rolling delight of stacked rock fences and shaggy hedgerows delineating pasture from ploughland, randomly punctuated by hewn stone cottages with thatched roofs, wooden outbuildings, and cows.

However, with a deep blanket of snow on the fields and treetops, and settling on the thatched roofs like woolly nightcaps, nature had raised the stakes considerably. Now, jolly puffs of smoke lingered above the cottages, telling of warm hearths and spirits within, field and meadow joined in fluffy, white conviviality, and the cows were all snug in their cow-houses. Or I assume they were, because there wasn't a living thing to be seen from my window to the horizon except, in due course, a great block of a policeman, shaped like two normal sized-policemen stacked sideways, behaving in a most peculiar manner.

The constable was taking, for his size, slow and graceful strides, tracing an invisible path between the grounds of Herding House and a squat structure of timber and thatching that peeked at us over the edge of a shallow dale. I took this to be Tannery Lodge, the home of Flaps Fleming. I idled at the window and watched the bobby in the snow, partially out of curiosity and partially because of the bucolic symmetry of a winter landscape observed from a deep leather armchair in a low, beamed-ceiling bedroom of stone walls, a four-poster bed, and a crackling fire in a pot-belly brazier.

The immense policeman would occasionally stoop to examine a compelling bit of snow and take note of it in his notebook, before continuing and eventually disappearing over the meadow's edge. By and by, he returned, performing the same staggered, fastidious examination of his route, and now that he was facing me I could see that he was a square-jawed, serious-faced chap who, having resigned himself to gingerhood, had gone all in and sprouted a wobbly great orange moustache.

"Constable Kimble," announced Puckeridge as I tapped down the rustic oak staircase to the main hall. In the doorway was a giant in royal blue with brass buttons, stamping snow off his boots with the energy and effect of one sinking piles for a railway platform. The foyer of Herding House, like most of the place, is of a hunting lodge aesthetic, and with each stomp the wagon-wheel chandelier shuddered, the wood-panelled walls creaked and their paintings of pastoral Hertfordshire bounced, and Puckeridge aged about a year.

"Compliments of the season," I said, offering my hand. The constable regarded me from a strategic advantage, high atop his shoulders.

"Mister Boisjoly, I presume."

"Live and in person for three nights only," I said. "We appreciate your prompt arrival, Constable. Anyone with the constitution of the average aunty would be understandably nonplussed by the situation, but my Aunt Azalea has a considerably lower than average tolerance for encountering dead bodies on Christmas morning."

"Christmas morning, you say, sir."

"It most certainly is, Constable. Which is why we're so grateful for your quick reply to the call of duty, but I suppose one day is much like any other on the thin blue line, all murder and mayhem and loitering with intent, what?"

The constable's eyebrows lowered magnificently, like resplendent boot brushes, and he fixed me with an analytical eye.

"I am aware of the date, Mister Boisjoly," he said. "What I wish to establish is the certitude of the recollection of Miss Boisjoly, vis-a-vis the time of day."

"She seemed quite certain when I spoke to her."

"Nevertheless, sir, I will be requiring the lady's statement in person."

"Might I ask why, Constable? She has quite pressing business with some drapery, at the moment."

"There was a heavy snowfall last night."

"I noticed," I said. "And I would like to take this opportunity to say how much I appreciate it. It's not really Christmas without a deep layer of the stuff, settling on thatched roofs like woolly nightcaps, etc., don't you think?"

"The consequence of a fresh snowfall, in the case of a death by suspicious circumstances, is that footprints are clearly demarcated and preserved."

"Handy, in police work, I should think," I said.

"It is indeed most helpful, sir," said Constable Kimble. "In the case of the death of Major Fleming, there are only two sets of footprints."

"Intriguing," I said. "Sounds like you're already hot on the trail of the killer. Whose footprints are they?"

"Those of the victim," said Constable Kimble, with some considerable gravity, "and those of your aunt, Azalea Boisjoly."

CHAPTER TWO

The Intrepid Interception of the Inevitable Inspector

"You made it, Vickers, just in the nick of tea-time."

My valet, refreshed from his rest in the Herding House laundry, had appeared at the door of the Heath Room, bearing a tarnished tray and a bewildered expression.

"Tea-time?" This was not out of character for Vickers. The man had been a pillar of the British valeting industry by that point for the better part of a century, and the pinions would intermittently pop a sprocket. It's a good job I'm not a man of routine, because Vickers would oft-times serve cocktails at sunrise and run my bath in lieu of preparing dinner.

"Tea-time, Vickers," I confirmed. "I offer, as exhibit A, the silver platter in your hands." Vickers looked down at the tray with some surprise, as though it had followed him from the kitchen of its own free will. "Which, I observe, is empty."

"I had the distinct impression that something was missing," said Vickers, looking at his reflection in the tray.

"No matter, Vickers. I would seek your counsel on matters more pressing."

"More pressing than tea, sir?"

"If you can imagine it. Tell me, what's the general disposition below-stairs at Herding House?"

"Herding House?" said Vickers. He relaxed his scrutiny of the tray and ventured into the room, taking it in like a tourist on Regents Street.

"We're at Herding House, Vickers," I reminded him. "We're visiting my Aunty Azalea."

"Of course. Herding House." Vickers locked the tray under his arm and assumed a military bearing. "The facilities and servants' quarters occupy the back half of the ground floor. Accommodations are very generous."

"You're not arm-wrestling Puckeridge for the top bunk, then."

"No, sir. My room is most commodious."

"I'm delirious to hear it," I said. "But in fact I was enquiring more about the mood among the staff, with particular emphasis on the untimely passing of Flaps Fleming."

"My impression is that Major Fleming was regarded, both here and throughout the village, as something of a local treasure." Vickers was gearing up, now, and had reached something nearing a cruising speed. The man had little capacity nor, so far as I could tell, interest in forming new memories, but his recollection of the distant past was encyclopaedic.

"Had you heard of him?"

"Oh, yes, sir," said Vickers. "Until very nearly the end of

the war the newspapers were rarely without some account of the major's daring."

"Very nearly?" I asked. "Had he lost interest as the war dragged into its fourth innings?"

"He was shot down over the channel, I believe, and was rescued at sea by Belgian fishermen. The ordeal cost him an eye."

"Rather a vital tool of the trade for a pilot, I would expect."

"My understanding is that the event expedited the major's retirement to private life."

"And the papers lost interest, did they?" I said. "Typical fickle Fleet Street."

"It was apparently the major's expressed wish to be left alone. He refused all manner of attention from the press."

"Most intriguing," I said. "Any idea why?"

"It's not uncommon for non-professional soldiers to be deeply affected by combat, and pilots in particular had a famously low survival rate."

"I expect he would have seen rather a lot of carnage for his age. Weren't fighter pilots typically recruited directly from the nurseries of the nation?"

"It was generally held that young men had quicker reflexes and more acute vision," confirmed Vickers. "The major, however, was approaching thirty years of age when he became a squadron leader, owing to his unique experience in Balloon Section."

"Sounds like a regular Allan Quartermain," I said. "And yet he retires to the life of a recluse while he's still got one good eye."

"Mister Puckeridge tells me the major had become increasingly social of late. He had developed a small but loyal group of acolytes at the local pub, and had recently been receiving visits from the vicar."

"And yet who should discover his body but my Aunty Azalea, who doesn't leave a house unless it's on fire," I said, looking out the window at Tannery Lodge. "This is the rummiest ingredient of this rum cocktail. My aunt is famously hidebound, what was she doing visiting an unmarried gentleman... in his home... without staff... he didn't have staff, did he, Vickers?"

"He lived entirely alone, sir."

"...without staff. This is very out of character. My father told me that she sent her regrets to every debutante ball from '85 until the beginning of the war."

"Miss Boisjoly displays an admirable consistency," said Vickers, somewhat absently, as he gazed about the room as an aid to orienting himself in space and time.

"You know, Vickers, this feudal spirit of yours is positively inspiring, sometimes."

"You're very kind to say so, sir."

"Don't mention it," I said. "Do you recall meeting my Aunty Azalea when she came down to Kensington for Christmas in '18?"

"It's possible the event slipped my mind."

"It's possible, but it didn't," I said. "You didn't meet her. She spent the entire visit in her room. I only encountered her myself on Christmas morning on the way to the bathroom, and even then she claimed to be an elf."

"Doubtless she wished to preserve the magic of the

moment."

"Vickers, I was eighteen years old."

"It is so that Miss Boisjoly is regarded, by some of the staff, as aloof," said Vickers.

"They do her a disservice," I said. "She achieved aloof by the age of ten. Before she was my age she was a full-on introvert. Now she's a master of disguise. She might be in this very room, even as we speak. Consequently, no-one can confirm when she went to Tannery Lodge nor how long she stayed there."

"That is my understanding."

"And now this Constable Kimble monument seems to think he can turn that, plus some vague depressions in the snow, into an airtight case for the prosecution."

"Most distressing."

"You know what I'm going to do, Vickers?"

"I wouldn't presume, sir."

"I'm going to go to Steeple Herding, that's what I'm going to do."

"Shall I pack your bags?"

"We're not leaving, Vickers. I have a duty to defend my aunt's innocence," I said. "I'm going to Steeple Herding station to intercept the inevitable Inspector from Scotland Yard."

"Will there be an inspector from Scotland Yard in Steeple Herding?"

"Inevitably," I said. "No country constable has the authority to investigate a suspicious death, and it's been several hours since the prodigious Kimble made his spurious discovery. By now he'll have wired to London for someone qualified by rank and aptitude to fit up Aunty Azalea for murder."

Henry, the boot and knife boy, was sent to fetch transportation. Vickers and I had come from Steeple Herding in a Wolesley war ambulance that had found a new lease on life as some sort of farm utility vehicle and occasional station taxi. Its better days were behind it, though, and when it reached the icy incline, still a good mile from Herding House, it shied with an unambiguous whirring sort of complaint, and the smell of well-cooked rubber.

I stood outside, contemplating the treacherous hillside, when Henry returned triumphantly from the pages of a Dickens novel, seated next to a large, avuncular, cloth-capped Little-John holding the reigns of a dappled grey Clydesdale and riding an open landau that had been converted, with the addition of two ingenious skis, into a sleigh, complete with silver bells.

"Compliments of the season, sir," sang the coachman with a smooth baritone that couldn't have accompanied the tinkling of bells and whinny of the horse better if it had been scored by Elgar. The boy hopped down from the sleigh, causing it to bounce and jingle as horse and driver puffed clouds of steam into the crisp, clear, winter scene.

"Mister Trevor Barking, sir," said Puckeridge, who had been waiting faithfully at my side. "Mister Barking is the village blacksmith."

"I'm very much obliged for the quick service," I said, pulling myself up onto the bench next to a broadly smiling

Barking. "I have pressing business with the next train from London."

"It's no bother at all, Mister Boisjoly. Got business of my own at the station, as it happens." Barking sang a short verse of "ho ho ho" in a tone and tempo that the horse understood as "about you get, hie for the station, sharpish," and we were off at a jangly gallop.

The road between Graze Hill and Steeple Herding was, at the best of times, ambiguous. Beneath a thick layer of snow, it became little more than a pleasant memory of springtime, and Barking and his giant horse chose their path on the strength of scenic value. Once down the hill from Herding House, we were drifting through a narrow dale formed of bluffs rising on either side, topped with an uneven fraternity of snow-cloaked evergreens. The hills flattened and the way narrowed as we entered the remaining forest which ticked and crackled the way sleeping wood will in the winter. Tall, skeletal poplar trees reached toward the washed-out cyan sky as though captured in the moment when they cast off their leaves and instantly regretted it. Holly and cypress poked shoots of green from beneath the snow, serving as a festive reminder that this wasn't only winter, it was also Christmas Day.

Barking sang another variation of his "ho ho ho" ditty which the horse translated into a subtle acceleration, and the bells jingled in merry accompaniment. The clean, chill air became a light breeze, and it stung the cheeks and watered the eyes and added a haze of blurry sentiment to the seasonal scenery. The increase in speed was in anticipation of an incline, and in a moment we reached the top of the hill that informally demarcated the twin towns of Graze Hill and

Steeple Herding, and a great expanse of snow-covered Hertfordshire hove into view like a panorama Christmas card. Little country cottages and barns dotted the silvery landscape, which in turn was divided into oblong fields and pastures by hedgerows hidden beneath deep drifts. The only movement was a long, fleecy chute of steam lingering above the railway tracks, and the locomotive from which it puffed.

"The four-thirty from London," said Barking, and then ho-ho-hoed us down the hill.

We arrived at the station just as the train was sighing away a head of excess steam, after which all was quiet in that wintry way that is somehow more than merely an absence of sound. The station was of the functional, red brick variety, but with a dollop of snow on top it looked like Santa's workshop, and indeed the main street of Steeple Herding, a bustling metropolis compared to Graze Hill, brought to mind the enchanted village where the elves live. We waited at the front of the station while, presumably, crowds of holiday visitors disembarked from the train.

"Did you say that you had a passenger to bring back to Graze Hill, Mister Barking?"

"Yes, sir," said Barking. He looked furtively about at the entirely deserted street of dark, snow-covered cottages. "It's a detective-inspector, up from London... there's been a murder."

"Let us not leap to conclusions, Mister Barking, there are any number of explanations for how a man might come to lie beneath a Christmas tree with a knife in his back. Might have been a freak gift-wrapping accident."

"I was unaware of the circumstances. Constable Kimble only told me to collect a detective-inspector."

18

"Well that's a happy coincidence," I said. "That's who I've come to meet as well."

"Do you know the inspector?"

"Not as such, no, but I've met the type," I explained. "Officious, bull-headed and career-minded. Probably smokes a pipe and takes his meals standing up at a lunch counter. He'll be anxious to have someone fitted up for the crime by Boxing Day, so you'll want to have a ready account of your recent activities. Did the constable happen to mention this inspector's name?"

"Wittersham, I believe."

"Ivor Wittersham?" I gave the knees a happy slap. "I withdraw my previous statement, Mister Barking, I do know the man. Everything else I said stands, of course, but the inspector and I have locked horns once before, and I can assure you of a scene of much joy and astonishment."

"You don't say, sir."

"Wouldn't surprise me if there were tears."

As though instructed by the stage manager, Detective-Inspector Ivor Wittersham, who recently came within a hair's breadth of convicting my old college chum Fiddles Canterfell of the murder of his uncle, appeared at the door of the station. He was dressed for winter as he was dressed for summer, when I last saw him, in a sidewalk-grey trench coat and low-brimmed fedora. His little leading-man moustache was more lopsided than ever, and he held an optimistically small travel case in his hand. There were no other passengers at all, and the three of us were the only people on the street, which was already darkening under the early winter evening.

"That's the inspector now," I said. "Stand by for an

emotional spectacle, Mister Barking. You may wish to have a kerchief on hand." I waved and tannoyed, "Hallo, Inspector."

Ivor glanced at me without apparent emotion, and then picked his way wearily and warily through the snow.

"Good afternoon, Mister Boisjoly," said the inspector. "Are you Barking?"

"Not at all," I said. "Merely excited to see you."

The inspector fixed me with a look that recalled his appreciation for extemporaneous witticisms, and so I downshifted and said, "A trifle disappointed, though. I assured Mister Barking here of a sentimental reunion, much like a scene from a *comédie larmoyante*, but in English."

"I fully expected to see you, Mister Boisjoly," said Ivor, climbing into the back of the landau. "Constable Kimble wired me the details, including the involvement of a Miss Azalea Boisjoly."

I hopped down into the snow and then joined the inspector on the passenger seats.

"It's an uncommon name, I grant you, but my aunt and I are hardly the last of the Boisjoly line. A great-uncle of mine, Captain Algernon Boisjoly, stood only last year in the Mossley bi-election, garnering a record-smashing zero votes."

"Did he not vote for himself?"

"That's the very point of the anecdote, Inspector," I said. "The poor man voted for the Independent Labour candidate, one Roland Lewis Boisjoly, no relation. So you see the value of resisting this urge to take all Boisjolys for a single sample."

"It was a question of probabilities," said Ivor, as Barking ho-ho-hoed his horse to action. "I was called away from home on Christmas day, to travel thirty-five miles in inclement weather to look into a suspicious death the principal suspect of which is someone named Boisjoly. I assumed the worst and, indeed, there you are."

"So I am," I conceded. "And it's just this matter of 'principal suspect' with which I take issue. My aunt did not murder anyone. She lacks the initiative. I'm not suggesting that we should all strive to emulate the character of your average killer, but one must admit that a certain degree of industry is among the chief qualifications. My Aunty Azalea is more the retiring kind. Wouldn't say boo to a goose, even if the goose had it coming."

"Constable Kimble seems to think the evidence quite conclusive."

"I know he does," I said. "But the constable hasn't yet had the advantage of my penetrating intellect, unlike you. The poor, misguided leviathan thinks that a few impressions in the snow amount to a capital case, overlooking the possibility that Major Fleming was dispatched sometime last night, or even earlier."

"It's Flaps Fleming that's been killed?" said Barking, swivelling like a barn owl.

"I'm afraid so," I said. "Did you know him?"

"Of course I know the major," said Barking. "And if he's dead he weren't killed last night. If he was dead any time before eleven, it must have been a ghost that stood us all a round of Christmas cheer this morning, me and half the village."

CHAPTER THREE
The Subtle Sign at the Scene of the Crime

The sun had been completely crowded out by evening and grey clouds by the time we returned to Graze Hill, and winter was expressing itself in the form of fat, dopey snowflakes that descended in slow twirls and bumped into one another as they went about their business. Ivor and I disembarked at the bottom of the hill beneath Herding House and Tannery Lodge, and Barking continued into the village, bubbling with the effervescent energy of the gossip with a shiny silver scandal.

We paused at Herding House, partially because it was along the way and partially to store Ivor's travel bag, and as I followed him back out into the snow I posed the question that had doubtless been on everyone's mind for hours.

"Do you mind if I have a look at the scene of the crime, Inspector?"

Ivor took out his pipe, tamped down the bowl, and stood watching the darkness descend on Tannery Lodge.

"I'm very much of two minds about that, Mister Boisjoly," he said, staggering the delivery as he lit his pipe. "In light of your contribution to the affair in Fray last summer, I'm inclined to either grant you some limited role in this enquiry, or have you arrested and held as a public nuisance until it's complete."

"I see," I said, joining Ivor in musing on the house beyond the hill. "Yes, I can easily see the strengths in both approaches. Any danger of a decision in the near term?"

"No, actually, Mister Boisjoly, I've elected to allow you to aid in the investigation, but keep in reserve the option of locking you up."

"A very gentlemanly compromise," I said, and we set out across the snow, following the tracks of Constable Kimble and, ostensibly, Aunty Azalea. The impressions were easily distinguishable, as the earlier set appeared to have been left by a slight, hesitant woman of a certain age, and the other by a heavyset man wearing snowshoes and carrying a cow in a hamper.

Tannery Lodge was a low, timber-framed, wattle-and-daub cottage that, at high noon on a simmering summer's day, would have been merely charming. On a darkening Christmas night, surrounded by a glistening white landscape, adorned with a thick cap of snow, and with windows glowing with the promise of a warm fire within, it looked like something the Brothers Grimm might have reserved for the exclusive use of gnomes.

We pushed open the door to an orange-hued room that met all expectations, with the notable exceptions of a colossus of a constable, and a dead body beneath a Christmas tree. The interior was otherwise largely to form — a comfortable salon that took up most of the house, a low, beamed ceiling under which Constable Kimble was compelled to stoop, a dying fire in the immense, rough stone fireplace, and a modest scattering of jumble-sale furniture and keepsakes on the walls and mantels.

"Constable Kimble?" said Ivor, losing his hand in that of the constable. "I'm Detective-Inspector Wittersham. This is Mister Boisjoly."

"We've met," said Kimble. His strong objection to my presence, in light of Ivor's rank, was limited to a single raised eyebrow of dissent. Having made his views clear, the constable gave us the abridged version. "The deceased is Major Aaron Fleming. Forty-five years old, retired from the military, lived alone, no known next-of-kin. Hero of the Great War. He was a flying ace, sir."

"Did you know the victim?" asked Ivor.

"Only distantly, sir," said Kimble, looking down at the body beneath the tree. "I introduced myself when he first moved to Graze Hill, and knocked on his door once or twice a year, in due course of business."

Ivor bent at the waist to get a fresh angle on the cadaver. "I take it all is as it appears?"

Major Fleming was a tall, thin chap, who approached middle age like a part in a Hollywood adventure. He had a trim moustache, silver sideburns, and of all things an eye-patch over his right eye. He was lying on his stomach in shirtsleeves, braces, and tweed trousers, and he had been neatly and fully subdued by a long, thin blade, like a bayonet, that extended from his back, right above where a hero's heart once beat.

"No sign of a struggle, sir," said Kimble. "It would appear

that the major welcomed the killer into his home, and was taken by surprise."

"Was that fire lit when you entered the premises?" asked Ivor.

"Are you asking me if I lit a fire in a crime scene, sir?"

"No offence intended. It's a cold night. I note, however, that as it's still burning now, it most likely was lit sometime this morning."

"I was just coming to that, sir," said Kimble. "Yes, the major certainly started or rekindled a fire this morning, probably prior to visiting the pub. There are tracks in the snow, leading from here to the Sulky Cow, a public house in the village. There are also tracks returning from the pub."

"So he left the fire unattended," noted Ivor.

"It seems that way, yes sir."

"Is that likely, Constable?" I asked. "This house and everything in it is made mostly of wood. For an ambitious errant spark, it would have been the work of an instant to reduce Tannery Lodge to Tannery Lump of Ash, Drifting in the Wind. Was the major known to be careless in his habits?"

"I couldn't say, sir."

"Carry on Constable," said Ivor. "What else have you determined?"

"When the deceased returned from the pub, he was visited by a Miss Azalea Boisjoly, as I mentioned in my telegram. Hers were the only other tracks."

I had heard this bit, and so I wandered the room, although occupied as it was with furniture, Ivor, myself, and Mount Kimble, the effect was very much like a leisurely stroll in a crowded telephone box. Nevertheless, I was able to get something of a feel for the character of the departed. There was no war memorabilia to speak of, for instance, and that corresponded neatly with what Vickers had told me about the major's distaste for matters martial. In fact, apart from a single photograph of five smiling young glamour boys in leather and silk, this might have been the household of a conscientious objector. I recognised Flaps in the team portrait; second from the left, the tallest and most strikingly handsome of the lot, winking roguishly at the camera as though he had licentious plans for it.

At odds with that pacific impression, however, were a large number of books on the abundant subject of human conflict. Mostly military histories, in fact, including all — with the exception of one very conspicuous volume — of the complete works of the colourful war correspondent, Charles à Court Repington.

There was also a door leading to an immaculate kitchen, and another giving way to a small, monastic bedroom.

"When was the most recent snowfall?" asked Ivor.

"Yesterday evening, sir. No one could have visited the house since then without leaving tracks."

"Have you taken a statement from Miss Boisjoly?"

"She admits coming here this morning," confirmed Kimble, "but claims it was sometime between seven-thirty and eight o'clock, and that the major was already dead when she arrived."

"And yet this Barking chap, the one who picked me up at the station, he swears that he had a drink with the victim this morning at around eleven o'clock," added Ivor.

"He's not alone in that," said Kimble. He withdrew his

26

police notepad and opened it to the latest page. "Several of what I understand are regulars of the Sulky Cow — Trevor Barking, Everett Trimble, and Cosmo Millicent, not to mention the landlady, Sally Barnstable — all state that the major stood them a Christmas round this morning between ten and eleven."

"Could Miss Boisjoly be mistaken about the time?"

"I would say that was self-evidently the case, Inspector," said Kimble with dark irony. "Either that, or she's being deliberately untruthful."

"I think you're overlooking a third explanation, Constable," I said.

"If you're referring to the possibility that the patrons of the pub were all mistaken, sir, I have already ruled that out. Sunrise is at eight o'clock. Miss Boisjoly claims that it was still dark when she visited Tannery Lodge."

"So what you're saying, if I read you correctly Constable, is that you subscribe to the theory that this morning, between the hours of ten and eleven, the village pub received a visit from none other than the ghost of Major Aaron Fleming. I applaud you, Constable, on your broad-minded views." I turned to Ivor. "No offence, Inspector, but this is the kind of progressive thinking that's lacking at Scotland Yard."

"No, sir," corrected Kimble. "That's not what I'm saying at all."

"Because ghosts don't make tracks in the snow?" I said. "They don't famously stand Christmas rounds, either, but we have to work with the evidence to hand."

"What is your aunt's relationship to the deceased, Mister Boisjoly?" asked Ivor.

"I couldn't say, really. Frankly, I'm surprised they had any sort of contact at all."

Kimble, however, had more to say on the matter. "Miss Boisjoly told me that she and the major had recently formed a friendship, the grounds of which were physical proximity and a mutual distaste for crowds."

"Did you find evidence of anything beyond a cordial acquaintanceship?"

"No, Inspector," said Kimble. "I think it stands to reason that anything in the way of love letters would have been destroyed by the suspect."

"If I may, Constable," I said. "I think I can see where you've gone wrong. It's in assuming that my aunt is the sort of woman to go in for these things you call 'love' and 'letters'. Nothing could be further from the truth."

"The murder was committed sometime since the last snowfall," said Kimble. "And the only tracks in the snow since that time are those of the victim and Miss Boisjoly."

"Have you another theory of the crime, Mister Boisjoly?" asked Ivor.

"I recognise I'm just a village constable, sir, and that you're a detective-inspector from London," said Kimble, with an implied 'la-di-da' prefixing the word 'London', "but might I enquire why it is that a civilian — a close relation of the chief and only suspect in a murder — is being consulted on said crime?"

"Fair question, Constable," said Ivor. "It's something akin to a debt of honour. Mister Boisjoly's intervention in another case this summer prevented a serious miscarriage of justice."

"I understand, sir," said Kimble, with a delicately

nuanced insubordination you don't expect from your simple country rozzer.

"Pure happenstance," I lied. "Plus I had the home-field advantage."

"Do you mean to say you're not familiar with the village and inhabitants of Graze Hill?"

"I've been here about half a day longer than you have, Inspector," I said. "So we're both starting on damp turf, and facing a particularly dodgy clubhouse turn in the form of an impossible murder with an impossible suspect."

"Am I to understand, then, that the sum total of your local knowledge amounts to the contention that your aunt is an unlikely murderer?" said Ivor.

"Surely narrowing the field of suspects is a contribution of incalculable value," I said. " But I also note a number of anomalies about the scene of the crime."

"Such as?"

"Did you notice, for instance, that the bed was neatly made, as though not slept in last night?"

"I took note of that detail," said Kimble. "The major was of a military background, and his day had already begun before he was killed. Doubtless he made the bed as a matter of daily habit before visiting the pub."

"Exactly," I said. "And yet, what about the fire?"

"It's already been observed that the fire was started this morning."

"Indeed," I conceded. "And then left unattended and, I observe, unkempt. Very unlike the rest of the household. The ash is overflowing, as though with the residue of something substantial, recently destroyed by fire."

"Such as a cache of love letters," said Kimble with the firm, exasperated tone of one giving an obvious answer for the second time.

"Possibly," I allowed. "But I would ask you to connect the two points — the house is in impeccable order, maintained by a man of military habits. Nothing out of place. No discarded clothing nor inexplicable dishware under the divan, no books propped up on the bedside table against a bottle of Calvados that Vickers brought me the night before. So where, then, is volume one of the war diary of Charles à Court Repington?"

"Who?" asked Kimble.

"Charles à Court Repington," I repeated. "Gentleman rogue and war correspondent, whose memoirs of the Great War are rather cynically entitled *The First World War,* as though he warmly anticipated a sequel." I stood aside like a curtain opening on the bookshelf and indicated the conspicuous absence in the otherwise orderly archive.

"Note the binding," I said, drawing the second volume from the shelf and holding it up for the appraisal of the court. "In particular, the brass corners. It is my contention that if you search those ashes you will find four identical ornamentations, referred to in the trade, unless I'm mistaken, as 'thingamabobs'."

Ivor and I turned our privileged attention on the constable, whose expressive eyebrows spoke of the pathos of a proud man obliged to perform a menial task.

"Right," he said and armed himself with a poker. He crouched before the fire and raked methodically through the ash. Within moments he stood and held up the poker, from which dangled the charred remains of a leather book jacket, still attached to a dull brass thingamabob.

"I'd have found that on my own in good time," said Kimble.

"Doubtless," I agreed.

"Now the question is, who put it on the fire," said Ivor.

"I think we'll find, Inspector, that the more revealing question is why."

CHAPTER FOUR
The Affair of the Phantom Farewell

The grim, early evening of winter is utterly stymied by snow. It's not for a lack of effort — a pale sun is chased from an ashen sky just after tea-time, and darkness does its level best to spread despair across the land. But then a silvery moon conspires with a blanket of purest white to reflect light and goodwill and a general spirit of holly and hope, stars twinkle in the velvet sky, a serene silence reigns, and whatever dark doubt that dusk was hoping to promote is quickly forgotten. The darkness is chased off to, I imagine, March, wherein to dream of rainy days in Spring.

The only sound breaking the silky, forest silence was a clumsy Boisjoly, crunching through the snow, having been ejected from Herding House. It was Ivor's view that I would be unlikely to make a constructive contribution to the hard questions he intended to put to my aunt.

The road from Herding House to the village centre of Graze Hill is a natural formation between the hill itself and a now frozen canal. The path was therefore distinguishable even and perhaps especially when covered with snow and the tracks of Barking's ingenious sleigh. I followed the road as it wound around the hill and after perhaps a mile the little cottages, pub, feed store and church that form the heart of Graze Hill came into view, framed by the night sky and lightly veiled with puffy snowflakes. Warmth glowed at the windows and lazy trails of grey smoke lingered above the chimneys, adding the rustic aroma of woodfire to the cold night air.

The Sulky Cow was a low structure of thatch and stone at the entrance to the wobbly main street. Snow was settled on the roof like a woolly hat and gathered like fluffy eyebrows above the window frames at either side of the door, giving the place the demeanour of a wise, old man reacting to surprising news. Beyond this friendly face was a welcoming orange glow and the pother and chatter of pub regulars.

The bustle silenced as I entered and two patrons and a barmaid looked to the door. Doubtless they expected one of their number, and they registered a theatrical, shared anticipation to receive a new entry in the *dramatis personae*, and the promise of a twist before the end of the first act.

"Compliments of the season," I said, and pushed the door firmly closed against the cold.

I might have drawn the tavern from memory without ever having been there. The stone of the exterior was also that of the interior walls, the low ceiling was formed of beams and rough planks of oak stained by the years, the furnishings were mismatched tables and milking stools, and the decor was delightfully amateurish watercolour renditions of pastoral Hertfordshire. In the left corner was an oak bar, worn to a warm, glowing finish by centuries of convivial elbows. The right wall was mostly occupied by a generous fireplace of whole found stone. A broad fire of split wood glowed and flickered, and an iron cauldron was suspended over it from a hinged and serrated chimney hook. Mulled wine simmered in the crock and filled the atmosphere with the scent of Christmas cheer.

"Are you that inspector from London?" asked the apple-cheeked woman behind the bar. She was of the full, robust, farm-bred type of woman — the sort who learn to pull a pint and yoke an ox at their mothers' knee. Barking was there, too, and he was sharing a low table and a large pint with a keen-faced chap of the sort engaged by the makers of shirt collars to appear in magazines holding a tennis racket or scrutinising a billiards table.

"You flatter me, madame," I said. "Inspector Wittersham is a dashing, Byronic figure, with eyes that flash with lightning intellect and a signature style irreproducible outside the very best mail-order catalogues. I am merely Boisjoly, nephew to Azalea, seeker of truth. Good evening Mister Barking."

"Evening, Mister Boisjoly," said Barking, raising his tankard in a toast of welcome. "May I introduce Sally-Ann Barnstable, landlady of the Sulky..." The apple-faced Sally-Ann smiled and waved from behind the bar. "...and this here is Everett Trimble, owner and operator of the feed store..." Everett squinted photogenically and gave me one of those 'both of us, men of the world' sort of nods. "...and that..." Barking gestured with his tankard toward an upholstered bench piled with a careless jumble of winter coats, "...is Soaky Mike."

The careless jumble of winter coats raised its head, revealing it to be a gentleman of advanced years and general air of dreamy contentment, as one who knows what he likes and where to get it. Soaky favoured me with a waggle of his white eyebrows and the lifting of a cup of mulled wine. As though to economise on the action, on the descent the cup stopped at his lips.

"It's an honour to ring in the season with you," I said. "Is that a communal cauldron of yule fuel?"

"Help yourself," said Sally, and put a clay tankard on the bar. I took it to the stove and ladled myself a cup of steaming wine, heady with distillation and cinnamon.

"Is Flaps Fleming really dead?" asked Sally.

"I fear so," I replied. "I've just come from viewing the remains. He looked very peaceful, apart from the knife in his back. I understand that he was surrounded by his dearest friends in his final hours."

"He was here this morning," said Sally, giving a brass beer tap a forlorn rub with a despondent dishrag.

"I should be very grateful of your recollections of this morning, as it happens." I leaned on the bar, implying a zone of confidentiality. "Was this morning's visit by special arrangement?"

"That's one bob for the wine, sir," said Sally. "Special arrangement?"

"It's Christmas," I said, withdrawing my change purse and putting a shilling on the counter. "Would you normally be open for business on Christmas Day?"

"The Sulky Cow is always open," said Sally with a resigned tone, as though long trading hours were an inescapable quality of the human condition. "Especially on Christmas. If it weren't for the Sulky, the entire population of Graze Hill would have nowhere to go at the best of times." Sally clasped my coin in her hand and, as she spoke this condemnation, her gaze settled on the three men in the bar. "You're looking, Mister Boisjoly, at the cream of village society. During the holidays, you see, Graze Hill evacuates all non-essential personnel. Those with farms are minding the cattle. Those without have gone to see in the season with family, so they'll be pasting bits of coloured paper together, I understand, and baking and eating mince pies."

"Are you saying that this is the entire Christmas contingent?"

"Very nearly. There's also Mister Padget, the vicar. He never comes to the pub, of course, but his houseguests are sometimes here."

"And Constable Kimble and the domestic staff at Herding House, presumably."

"We get that Mister Puckeridge in from time to time, but the constable only comes round at the end of the day, to remind us when it's past locking up."

"So who was here this morning when the major paid his visit?"

"Them three, of course," said Sally with a gesture of the chin toward the league of leading citizens. "And the vicar's houseguests; Flaps' nephew — bloke named Cosmo Millicent — and some posh bloke with one of those names that don't know where to stop; Monty McMontague-Mount-Muckity, or some such."

"Was that the major's usual cronies?"

"No, thank goodness," said Sally. "In the summer they were up to the rafters. Flaps telling his stories of daring in the skies over Belgium, his congregation buying him rounds and putting it on the cuff."

"I understand he was quite the hero."

"Don't I know it," said Sally, nodding earnestly. "Major Fleming is spoken of very highly within these walls, most particularly by Major Fleming." In the next instant Sally, who had been gazing idly at the barroom, raised herself to her full height, pointed at a scrappy tin pub clock on the wall next to the bar and spoke a clear, unambiguous, "Tut tut."

The meaning of this "tut tut" idiom appeared to be as plain to Soaky Mike as "ho-ho-ho" was to Barking's Clydesdale. He glanced at the clock and acknowledged that some agreed period had yet to elapse, and so sheepishly returned the ladle to the cauldron of wine.

I could understand the appeal to the discerning souse. The Sulky Cow clearly took a capacious approach to the preparation of its mulled wine and wasn't the sort of establishment to sink the ship for a penn'orth of rotgut rum. The base wine may at one point have been a drinkable merlot but it was diluted beyond recognition with cloves, anise, cinnamon, Spanish rum and a silt of orange peels and sultanas. All that, distilled all day over a low heat, had produced a lively dichotomy of sweet and stupefying. It put me in mind of a holdover evening of the all-night debating society at Balliol when we ran entirely out of, in chronological order, beer, wine, and Pimm's, and were faced with the stark choice of calling it a draw or mixing an antique china vase full of cooking sherry and pineapple juice.

"So, what do you make of this business with the

footprints?" I asked, swinging my attention back to Sally. She, however, kept her warden's scrutiny on Soaky Mike, who was affecting to be deeply distracted by the conversation between Barking and Everett.

"Footprints?"

"In the snow," I clarified. "I would have thought that Constable Kimble would have mentioned his novel theory about impressions in the snow."

"The constable's very professional. He doesn't go talking to anyone about police business."

There was something vaguely judgemental about the way she emphasised "he", as though it was meant to stand in stark contrast to "thee".

"I have a special dispensation," I pleaded. "I'm neither a policeman nor a professional. What did he tell you, then?"

"He asked who was here this morning and when, just like you did."

"It's not as though he holds the copyright."

"And then that inspector will come round and ask the same thing all over again. Doesn't seem fair to the poor man," continued Sally on an arc that had clearly been under development for some time. "No one's ever happy to see the local plodder until they need him, and even then when he finally gets a proper crime to solve — a murder, no less — they send some pompous, puffed-up detective-inspector up from London."

"I thought you hadn't met Inspector Witterhsham."

"Just don't think it's right, is all," said Sally, somewhat wistfully. "Just because a chap's big, that doesn't mean he's not bright. And he's not so big as all that.

"Quite right," I conceded. "Well within the advisable range. Bigger than a breadbox, smaller than the 16:42 from Charing Cross."

"Just about the right size for a policeman, if anyone's asking me."

"You'll be the first person I consult, next time the question arises," I assured her. "Did Constable Kimble say all this to you?"

"He might have alluded something, yes," said Sally, guardedly. "He's actually very sensitive, you know. Like a big old bear."

"A most apt comparison. I understand the Alaskan Kodiak is especially sensitive to condescension. What else did the constable say?"

"He asked when was the last time Flaps was in the Sulky Cow."

"Very astute," I said. "What was the answer?"

"Weekend before last. The major has — had, I suppose — a marked preference for the Saturday morning, pre-lunch audience," said Sally. "Gave him a chance to really sink his teeth into a story, get in a few rounds, and be on his way before anyone can suggest ordering food, say, or settling any outstanding bar tabs."

"Did Flaps have a particularly impressive line of credit?"

"He did," said Sally, meditatively, "and now he doesn't. This morning he stood everyone a round, which was already a first, and then in a single lump he closed out his bill. Nearly thirty quid."

"Was that very out of character?"

"Not wishing to speak ill of the dead," said Sally

graciously, "I'll just say that he was cheaper than change for a farthing, and leave it at that."

"Very diplomatic. What sort of humour was the major in this morning?"

"That's a question better put to his following," answered Sally with a nod to the men gathered around the stove.

"Then that is precisely where I'll put it," I said. "Please allow the Boisjoly trust to sponsor the next several lashings of comfort and joy." I put a crown on the worn and warm countertop and schooned into the low, cosy bar room.

"Welcome to Graze Hill, Mister Boisjoly, very much obliged, sit here, by the fire," said the shirt collar advertisement as I ladled out refills of wine. "Trimble's the name, call me Everett, everyone does. It's true, what Trevor here, Mister Barking, says, I run the feed store, and it's a dashed fine sideline, even if I'm saying it myself, but I'm alderman for Graze Hill, it's a calling, if I may, and someone's got to do it, wouldn't you agree, Mister Boisjoly, may I call you, erm?"

There was a jaunty, bouncy quality to Everett's narrative, not unlike the sensation of being in a small boat in choppy seas. I found myself following his line of thinking like a harried Christmas shopper running alongside a Route Six to Oxford Circus, trying to hop aboard.

"Anthony," I finally caught up. "Anty to my critics and fans alike. It's my very great pleasure, Everett. Topping bit of landscape you have here in Graze Hill. Just the sort of countryside you want on hand when visiting maiden aunts."

"And you're seeing it in the dead of winter, under two

feet of snow and without the electric hum of an industrious heartland," said Everett, taking up the theme and salting it liberally. This was his patch and I wasn't going to take issue with the words he chose to describe it, but this was the first I'd heard of dairy country humming electrically. "Having said that, you get the off-season advantage, without the rush of tourists and press of gawkers at the museum. Have you seen the museum, Anty? It's in the transept of the church. Fascinating collection of reliquary, including something that may very well be a string from Saint Dunstan's harp. Hard to say anything, with scientific certainty, about a bit of string, but it's an inspiration to behold, nonetheless. If it's science, you're after, you'll want to meet our Hildy — she's unlike anything you've ever seen before, Anty, that I can guarantee you. A wonder of nature. Got the best minds utterly baffled."

"Hildy?"

"A cow," answered Barking, who appeared to have been prepared for the question.

"Not just a cow," admonished Everett. "A Graze Hill Golden. Good for three and half gallons a day, yet she doesn't stand four feet tall, and she's native to the area. If you'll promise to keep it under your hat, Anty, I can tell you with some confidence that we fully expect Hildy to be recognised as a unique and authentic breed, possibly as early as next year. Wouldn't that be a glorious beginning to the new decade?"

I hadn't time to give my oath of secrecy before he blurted it out, so I made a silent promise to myself that if anyone were to discover this blockbuster before its natural due date, it wouldn't be from me. We raised our cups in a toast to Hildy the midget dairy cow.

"Dreadful business this," Everett geared down, now, and gave me the Eyebrow of Serious Business. "Local boy, you know, Flaps Fleming, grew up right on the hill. Learned his love of flight jumping into bales of hay from the loft window of the family barn with his mother's parasol. Have you seen some of the barns in Graze Hill, Anty? Magnificent craftsmanship. Asset to the town — Flaps, I mean, not the barns. Although there are some extraordinary examples — the Biggins operation, for instance, built on a stone foundation dating back to Guthrum, probably, two storeys high and with a cupola that would put you in mind of Saint Paul's. I had plans for Flaps, though, quite ambitious plans. Isn't that right, Trev?"

Barking gave a start on recognising his name in the din, and recovered too late to speak for himself.

"Statue of the local hero," continued Everett. "Trevor here is making it in his smithy. Bronze. Life size. Full uniform. Scarf valiantly flapping in the wind. Right out there..." Everett nodded toward the curtain of snow at the window. "...in the centre of town. Flaps was going to be guest of honour at the official unveiling in the spring. Dignitaries from all over, newspapers, wireless, wouldn't surprise me if the affair were to attract the attention of Buckingham Palace. I suppose that's all off, now. So, how about this murder? What's all this about footprints? Extraordinary legal mind, Constable Kimble. Like a steel trap. Dashed silly sending a detective-inspector up from London when there's a top-flight criminologist already on the job, I say. Coals to Newcastle, if you take my meaning."

"I most certainly do," I said, while Everett was drawing a quick breath. "He was very fastidious in the matter of the

42

footprints in the snow, following them from Tannery Lodge to the Sulky Cow, and back again. I believe he may have measured them, and appraised their quality and workmanship. It was his conclusion that the major must have made the return journey before being murdered."

"As opposed to?"

"As opposed to after," I said. "He didn't strike you as vaguely ephemeral, by any chance? Or display an uncharacteristic penchant for plaintive wailing?"

"Not noticeably, no," said Everett, with a confirmatory glance at Barking. "Trev?"

"Solid as ever, I'd say. Perhaps even more so," claimed the blacksmith.

"Was there anything unusual about him at all?"

The men shared another common thought and then both fixed me with that puzzled expression that Londoners reserve for tourists who pronounce the H in Thames.

"Of course," said Everett. "Like Sally just said, he bought a round of drinks."

"More than one," added Barking.

"Paid off his bar tab, in a single stroke," continued Everett. "And then, just before he left, he shook everyone's hand and wished us all a merry Christmas."

"And, to each of us, one at a time," said Barking, "he said goodbye... forever."

CHAPTER FIVE

The Mysterious Meeting in the Manger at Midnight

"Forever?" I said. "Just like that? Flaps Fleming said merry Christmas, goodbye forever, and then went home to be murdered?"

"Precisely so," confirmed Everett. "Well, not precisely like that. Not much like that at all, now you ask for the transcript. It was different for each of us, but something along the lines of, my time has come, I hope you'll always remember me, that sort of thing, wouldn't you say Trev?"

"Yes, I..."

"Of course, that's it, isn't it?" Everett snapped his fingers. "A memorial. It's just the thing. You'll have to accelerate the statue, Trevor. Maybe the scarf doesn't need to wave so valiantly as all that, if it'll shave a day or two off delivery. I trust you with the details..." Everett waved away the details that appeared to be on the tip of Barking's tongue. "...knock it together like you did the golden calf. Have you seen the golden calf, Anty? Absolutely dazzling. Have a look when

44

you come to church tonight. Tip-top of the clocktower. Solid bronze, not actual gold, of course, that would be exorbitant and, to hear the vicar tell it, heretical, but he's not a man of vision. Captivating orator, but not a man of vision. Bronze wasn't exactly free for the having either, in point of fact, but how can you put a value on a church weather vane immortalising the Graze Hill Golden? What was it before, Trev? Tin? Can't have that. You can see the tin cow in the church museum. Talking of which, gentlemen..." Everett cast an accusing eye at the clock, as though blaming it for the finite nature of time. "...I must be making arrangements with Mister Padget."

Everett drained his cup, whooped his farewells while wrapping himself in a big leather and wool overcoat, and swept out the door. Sally followed him, as one familiar with the practice, and pushed the door fully closed against the cold night air.

"A golden calf?" I said to Barking. "And a bronze pilot? You're a multi-layered man of mystery, Mister Barking."

Barking kept his eye on the door, as though without careful watching it might at any moment spill forth with another instance of Everett Trimble. "I believe that Everett thinks of it as a natural progression. My father was blacksmith to Graze Hill, and it was he who made the original tin cow weather vane for the church, some twenty-five years ago. This summer I was commissioned to replace it — elevate its profile, in Everett's words — with a solid bronze replica."

"A natural stepping-stone, I should think, from making shoes for horses to casting bronze memorials for local heroes."

45

"I suppose," said Barking, dubiously. "If that's where a man's natural talents should take him. But I'm more of the industrious type. Enterprising, you might say."

"I admire that, Mister Barking. This country needs its men of vision, like you and Mister Trimble, and it needs them to not be shy about it, like you and, with knobs on, Mister Trimble."

"Oh, yes?" said Barking, newly inspired by something. "Is that really your view?"

"It most certainly is, Mister Barking. It's no good hiding one's ambition under a bushel. I knew a chap at Oxford — Rickets, we called him, but I can't think of why at the moment, I'll have to get back to you on that — retiring as an ageing vicar. The sort of shrinking violet that the judgemental generation regard as a 'good influence'."

"I know the type well," said Barking, as one impatient to move a story ahead.

"Then you'll be as astonished as we were, Mister Barking, to learn what I, along with Melting Entwhistle-Hardy and Fiddles Canterfell, discovered during a stagger across the river to Oxford's seamy underbelly, otherwise known as the suburb of Cowley." I took a dramatically extended draw on my cup of merry mead, and then continued the tale of the ingenious Rickets, "Who there should we encounter but Rickets? We didn't know him straight away, lurking in an alley in a broad-brimmed hat and raincoat, like the sort of cove who goes about spy thrillers saying things like 'the rooster crows at midnight', and I daresay he didn't recognise us, either, because out of the shadows he asks if we're interested in taking art classes."

"Art classes? I don't know that's quite what I'd describe

as vision, Mister Boisjoly."

"You wouldn't? No, well, what if I were to tell you that he was asking and expecting no less than two pounds a student — per class, mind you."

"Well that's just where a man of vision can go wrong, sir." Barking raised an instructive finger and adopted a professorial tone. "Your friend priced himself out of the market. I don't know much about art, and I expect I know even less about Oxford, but I can tell you this — setting the right price is all a matter of knowing your market." Barking gave a furtive glance at Sally, who remained resolutely indifferent to us. "Take the Sulky Cow — a shilling? For a cup of hand-mixed mulled wine? At Christmas? They could ask two and six and no one would blink an eye. Let me set the prices of this pub and I'd turn it into a gold mine."

"I daresay you would, Mister Barking, but you misunderstand me," I said. "It wasn't an art class in the classical sense, or, rather, it was, perhaps even more so. Rickets was offering what are known as life drawing classes — eight chaps sitting about behind easels, chip of charcoal optional, gaping at a young lady striking artful poses in nothing but a spirit of good sportsmanship. Technically well within the law and, what with two classes Friday and Saturday evenings and a matinee on Sunday, quite lucrative."

"Surely you didn't pay the two quid, sir."

"Of course not, Mister Barking, we were students of Oxford University," I said with wounded school pride. "Rickets gave us the fellowship discount. Very enlightening experience, though it was months before we could look the chaplain's wife in the eye again."

"Yes, a very original enterprise, that," conceded Barking.

"Not the sort of thing people go in for, here in Hertfordshire, I don't think."

"More of a landscape crowd, are they? I'm unsurprised. Lovely countryside."

"What I meant was that my ambitions incline more toward the industrial, if you see what I mean."

"I may as well confess to you, Mister Barking, that I do not."

"Take for example, electro-plating," said Barking in what I received as an almost Everett-like detour. "Are you familiar with electro-plating, Mister Boisjoly?"

"Some sort of efficiency device for the modern kitchen, is it?"

"Electro-plating is the very latest advancement in the rendering of high-durability materials with a sleek, contemporary veneer."

"I say, that sounds jolly useful," I said. "Can't think of what it might be useful for, just at the moment, but it must come in tremendously handy."

"Very much so, yes. When used to apply a layer of chromium to the bumper of an automobile, for example, it reduces corrosion of the underlying metal, and gives the whole vehicle a smart, twentieth-century finish."

"Rather a departure from blacksmithing, I would have thought."

"May I confide in you, Mister Boisjoly?"

"I would have you think of me as an old chum, Mister Barking."

He looked furtively about. Soaky Mike was absorbed in the practice of running a finger around the interior of his cup and licking it, and Sally was at the door, putting on a coat and hat.

"Trev, don't let Soaky near bar nor kettle before that..." The landlady pointed at the pub clock, a gift from Albion Gin Distillers, commemorating a pre-war FA Cup final. "...says seven-fifteen. Understood?"

The commanding nature of pub landladies in general and Sally Barnstable in particular had both Barking and me taking careful note of the current time — seven o'clock — and committing to memory that which we could and could not do between then and quarter past. With a nod and rush of winter air, Sally was gone.

"One of the many things I admire about the countryside..." I said. "...the trusting nature of your publicans. A London landlord wouldn't leave his counter unattended to whisper a final oath to his dying mother."

"She's not going far," said Barking. "In any case, should anything go missing it's not as though there would be a lot of suspects."

"Something in that," I concurred. "That appears to be a universal truth of Graze Hill at Christmas."

"And she's only gone to milk Hildy."

"Do you mean to tell me that Hildy is an actual cow?"

"Of course," said Barking. "What did you think?"

"I assumed that Hildy was one of those collective monikers, like Johnny Foreigner or Constable Plodder. I didn't realise there was a working prototype."

"No, she's real enough. You can have a visit if you like — she's got her own stable behind the pub. Sort of the Sulky Cow mascot."

"I'll be counting the moments," I said. "But you were interrupted, I believe, as you were about to confide in your old Anty Boisjoly."

"I was." Barking eyed Soaky, who replied with the mischievous smile of the fifth form student who finds himself, suddenly and unexpectedly, under the naive watch of a substitute Latin master. "If you're interested in making a modest investment in a sure thing, I may be able to make room for another backer in my chromium-plating venture."

"Very kind of you, Mister Barking," I said. "At the moment most of my capital is tied up in racetrack debentures and whisky futures."

"Quite sure? Frankly, I could use a little nudge over the edge. Research and development has not proceeded as smoothly as hoped."

"Quite sure. It's my belief that bumpers, even those plated in chrome, will one day soon be rendered obsolete by safe driving and careful adherence to the posted speed limits."

"If you find the new technologies daunting," said Barking, lowering his chin and his voice ever further, "perhaps you'd be interested in another initiative of mine. Are you aware of the leisure trend which is sweeping the United States at the moment?"

"Bathtub gin?"

"The yo-yo."

"Remind me," I said. "Light rum, crushed ice..."

"It's a children's toy, Mister Boisjoly. A very successful and yet deceptively simple device formed of a wooden bobbin and a length of string. They're selling them by the trainload in America."

"I'm unsurprised," I said. "I was in New York, once. People were lining up on Fifth Avenue to pay five cents for a boiled frankfurter from a man selling them out of a tin drum. I believe that Americans will buy anything so long as someone else buys one first."

"You'd agree, then, that what's needed is a gimmick," said Barking, rounding to the other side of the table, possibly to prevent me from making a break for the door. "And that's just what I've got. You see, in America, they've got these travelling yo-yo demonstrations. I propose to do the same here. Soon, every child in Britain will want one, and with a little working capital, say, ten thousand pounds, I can ramp up production and meet that demand."

"Then I congratulate you, sir," I said, raising my cup of mulled wine. "Particularly if, to you, ten thousand pounds is a little working capital. To me ten thousand pounds is eight months to a year of well-rehearsed debauchery."

"The thing is..." Barking leaned back and drummed his fingers distractedly on the table, as though struggling with some weighty, internal deliberation. "...The thing is, with the passing of Major Fleming, I've lost my most important backer."

"Flaps Fleming was going to give you ten thousand pounds to manufacture yo-yos?"

"Five thousand, if I'm being completely transparent with you," confided Barking transparently. "With five thousand in reserve, should the pace of production need to be increased."

"Strangely risk-averse, for a flyboy," I observed. "Weren't you a little dismayed, then, when he bade you farewell forever?"

Barking tipped up his cup and examined the remains. He plucked a raisin from the dregs and popped it into his mouth.

"You win some, you lose some, as the Americans say," said Barking, now preoccupied with sifting the silt in his cup.

"Yes, as a nation it's an endless source of penetrating philosophy," I said. "I'm surprised to learn that Flaps had the means. Tannery Lodge strikes me as the cosy, unpretentious sort of abode preferred by men of undemanding tastes and limited resources."

"Oh, no," said Barking, with renewed interest. "He was the last of a line that still collects tribute on most of the farmland in Graze Hill and Steeple Herding. It just happens the major preferred to live modestly, out of the public eye."

"Far from the madding crowd's ignoble strife, along the cool sequestered vale of life," I paraphrased shamelessly. "Not sure I see the appeal, myself. I don't know that I'd go through the whole bother of being shot down over open seas if there wasn't at least a little madding crowd in it for me."

"I think the major was coming round to that way of thinking himself." Barking drained his cup and then rose from the table. "I'm afraid that I've got to be going — on top of everything else I'm expected to do, I'm verger of Saint Stephen's, and there are hymn books and wine and wafers to be laid on before Eucharist."

"Eucharist?" I asked. "What Eucharist?"

"Holy Communion," said Barking. "Mister Padget goes in for the whole wine and crackers. We even do incense, while we've got supplies in."

"I know what Eucharist is, Mister Barking, but didn't all that get sorted out this morning?"

"Not in dairy country." Barking spoke 'dairy country' as though it was a widely-established synonym for 'wasteland'. "No one has time to come to church in the mornings. Services start tonight at ten."

The blacksmith clad himself in lambswool and leather and made for the door. "I hope you'll give my proposition careful consideration, Mister Boisjoly. 'Til tonight, gentlemen."

A cold breeze swept quickly in and just as quickly back out again, taking Barking with it, and I was alone with a smiling, wobbling Soaky Mike. He waggled his eyebrows meaningfully at the clock.

"Quite right," I said, relieved to note that the eyebrows were bang on the bell. "Allow me." I ladled a generous portion of steaming glog into Soaky Mike's cup, to my own disadvantage because little remained of the brew but a squishy deposit of citrus peelings and dried fruit.

"I'm afraid that's the last of it," I said, lowering myself onto a milking stool on the other side of the open fire from the old man.

"There's whisky behind the bar," he countered. Or he may have contended that there were "sixty beside the barn" or that it was plainly "risky to blind the tzar", for the man spoke without the slightest hint of an upper palate, but with a winking, beguiling charm that made whatever he was proposing sound like a jolly conspiracy.

"I daresay you're right," I conjectured. "But let us content ourselves with what nature provides and Sally Barnstable will allow. Do I understand it that you were here this morning to benefit from the largesse of Flaps Fleming?"

"Arum," said Soaky, earnestly. "He give me a whisky when he come, and another when he goed."

"And this was out of character, you'd agree?" I was beginning to pick up on the unique cadence of Soaky's personal dialect.

"Bloke was tight as a lady's slipper on a Clydesdale."

"Very colourful. And did he also bid you a fond forever farewell?"

"That he did. And very pretty it was, sir. Soaky, he said, I never give you more than a passing thought, never, but I believe that, someday, I may well do so again."

"How moving."

"Arum."

The door burst open with a crisp intake of wind and Sally bustled into the bar, and then leaned back against the door, pushing it closed. She cast a dubious eye over the touching scene as she removed her big woollen mittens.

"All correct and timely," I assured her. "And that's the last of the elixir."

"That works out well," said Sally, unwrapping herself. "It's time I was closing up, now."

Sally busied herself momentarily behind the bar while Soaky savoured the last of his wine, and then she approached the fireplace. She lifted the cauldron off the chimney hook and prepared to sling the remains onto the fire but I stopped her, acting on what would turn out to be a far more consequential whim than I could possibly have anticipated.

"You're not discarding all that high-calibre sediment, surely?"

Sally looked into the cauldron and then back up at me, as

54

though I'd just enquired after the fate of her eggshells and coffee grounds.

"You want it?"

"I most certainly do," I confirmed. "There's no better base for a pot of mulled wine than the remains of a previous pot of mulled wine, and I have well-grounded suspicions that this is one of many Christmas traditions which my aunt will overlook. *Entre-nous,* I won't be very surprised if she's forgotten to lay on dinner."

We three exchanged those warm assurances one feels compelled to convey on a dark Christmas evening that we eagerly anticipated seeing one another at church, and I was back in the crisp winter night.

I had been in the pub perhaps forty-five minutes, during which the scenery had been touched up with glitter and relit with a carefully positioned silvery spot. A fresh fall of snow scintillated where it lay and twinkled as more fell in slow, drunken trajectories against the darkness. I was enveloped once again in that inimitable silence afforded by the singular sound-absorption qualities of snow, and the magical fog of my own breath and the cauldron of hot raisins in my hand. In short, it was an enchanted moment to be alone.

Ahead of me lay the path home. An excellent choice, but lacking the promise of serendipitous moments and rather heavy with the promise of regaining Herding House before time. The other way lay Greater Graze Hill, with an unblemished blanket of snow, quiet, glowing cottages, and, it had just occurred to me, an actual living specimen of the Graze Hill Golden. Swinging my bucket like Little Red Riding Hood, I crunched through the snow toward the rear of the Sulky Cow.

I fell immediately into darkness. A small alley was formed between the pub and a low wooden manger. The space was narrow and crooked and the moon had difficulty finding it. I stopped in the darkness, partially because I didn't know where the manger door was but mostly because my steps were echoing in a most suspicious manner. Somebody was following me. When I stopped the echo stopped, just slightly out of time, and when I continued it started up again. I stared hard into the shadows but the contrast against the moonstruck snow rendered them as the depths of an oil well. I could see my own footprints beyond the entrance to the alley, though, and they were no longer alone.

There's something about still, silent winter nights that gives flight to the imagination, and I had little difficulty conjuring a vivid image of a knife-wielding madman, approximately six foot two, dark complexion, scar above the left eye, cauliflower ear, descended brow, and a subtle but unmistakable look of what I guess one would call a yearning. I turned on my heel and made for the light.

Once around the corner I was inspired, possibly by the sound of footsteps in quick pursuit, to continue around the manger. I turned the next corner and noted, in passing, the entrance, but banked the knowledge for some later enterprise. At the moment, I felt that my energies were best employed in dashing through the snow.

As I rounded another corner it occurred to me that I was being chased in a circle around the manger, and while I was quite confident in my ability to run literally all night if necessary, I also realised that the next turn into the darkness of the alley and a heavy iron cauldron in my hand presented the best I could hope for in terms of a last stand.

I stopped in the darkness and put my back to the wall of the manger. This positioned the cauldron in my left hand, so I broke against the back leg and prepared to bowl a googly the moment my murderer hove into view.

Nothing. Not the sound of mad, lunging footfalls in the snow nor even the feral snorts of a blood-thirsty killer. I calmed my own breathing and heartbeat, in the manner of what I imagine is that of the professional soldier or primary school teacher, and listened.

It was barely a tic, a stitch of sound, sharply expelled, and it was behind me: "Hic."

I spun on the spot. My feet were solidly embedded in the snow, though, so I twisted like a damp dishrag. The cauldron bounced off the wall of the manger and fell into the snow and then I, robbed of even the dubious benefit of the graceless stagger, followed.

"Pox and spells, Soaky, you very nearly frightened me to death."

Soaky Mike smiled impishly in the darkness.

"Thought you might be wanting of company."

"Is that your idea of companionship? Stalking people in the dark? It's a good job Mister Bell had Tom Watson on hand for his breakthrough rather than you, or we'd all be answering the telephone with a hearty 'gaaahh!'"

"Didn't know you was so skittish."

"Well, I'm happy of the opportunity to set you straight on the point — I am." I grasped Soaky's hand and he pulled me from a Boisjoly-shaped indentation in the snowbank.

"My apologies."

"No, no, my fault," I said, reflecting on the simple fact

that it was. "I suppose you were after the remains of the mulled wine."

We looked down at the cauldron, which had spilled its guts onto the snow. The effect of blood red wine and slushy fruit splashed against the sheet of white made the cauldron look as though it had come to a violent end.

"I don't suppose you'll be wanting it now," said Soaky, scooping the frosty remains back into the cauldron.

"I'll take that," I said, doing so. "Perhaps some sort of frozen dessert can be rescued from the debacle. In any case, I have no intention of inviting the disfavour of Sally Barnstable. I have a vague fancy that you feel the same."

"Arum."

"Then let no more be said about it," I said. "Now show me this cow that's got the bright set talking."

The interior of the stable was balmy, compared to the cold night outside, and it was dimly lit by glowing embers in an iron brazier. The room smelled of straw and earth and the robust scent of large herd animals in their natural habitat. The effect transported me, briefly but fully, to the Juniper Gentlemen's Club during cocktail hour.

The little manger was a dedicated suite of rooms for its single VIP occupant. Separating man from animal was a low, simple wooden barrier, on one side of which was a barrel of feed and on the other a long trough. As we entered, the most peculiar animal I'd ever seen looked up from dinner.

Her enormous, brown, bovine eyes met mine and I was instantly charmed by her projected good nature, as though she was saying, in a glance, 'Look here, I know we've never met but I can't help feeling that we're going to be jolly good mates, you and me.' There was nothing unusual in that, of course — most beasts of field and foyer tend to grant me an *a priori* fellowship. What was odd about this particular fully grown cow was the way she looked *up* at me. Stranger still, the Graze Hill Golden is, apparently, a perfectly normally proportioned breed of cow — generous of haunch and with a comfortable, jowly countenance — but with stubby legs like a dachshund. She wouldn't have been more than four feet tall in high heels. She was also uniquely stamped — apart from a dusting of white about the snout and ears, Hildy the midget cow was of a warm, coppery tone, not unlike the moustache of Constable Kimble.

"Hello Hildy," I said with sincere amity. "Merry Christmas."

Judging by her response, this was the first she was hearing that today was noteworthy, and if Hildy had already found in me a solid ally and friend she sealed the deal with her response, which was to dance excitedly from side-to-side, stamping her left and right hooves in alternating rhythm. I was seized by a desire to communicate my appreciation of this sincere bonhomie in a manner a creature of such sweet simplicity could understand and, not coincidentally tiring of my duty of care for an iron bucket of saturated orange rinds, I emptied the cauldron into the trough. Hildy's eyes widened with feeling and then she set about the offering with a relish that I can only describe as moving.

"You'd have been better letting me have that, Mister Boisjoly," said Soaky petulantly.

"I rather thought you might think that," I said. "And so I've relieved you of temptation, you can go to your bed with a pure heart. *Pax vobiscum.*"

"You misjudge me," insisted Soaky. "I only followed you out to tell you something about Major Fleming. Something I'll bet you a pint to a penny you don't know."

"I didn't know who he was before this morning, Soaky. I imagine there are volumes I don't know about the man."

"But this, no one else knows neither," said Soaky. "Major Fleming, whatever else he might have been, he weren't no hero."

CHAPTER SIX

The Candid Revelations of the Christmas Celebrations

Soaky Mike left me with that cryptic thought and disappeared into the night. I stood blinking after him, and might have given chase had Hildy not said "Moo" in that peculiar way some cows have of saying "moo" as though they're reading it as written. Her meaning, in its purest sense, was simple benediction, but I took it as a reminder that I had a duty to a maiden aunt who at that very moment had doubtless been chased deep into the drapery by the ham-handed tactics of Inspector Wittersham.

"Right you are, Hildy old thing," I said and bade her a merry Christmas night.

Herding House glowed a 'welcome home' amber against the 'no, stay outside and throw snowballs at the chimney' blue of the winter night. Puckeridge opened the door and I stamped into the warm, well-lit foyer in the primitive dance performed by all who are plagued by snow clinging to their trouser-cuffs.

"What ho, Puckeridge," I said. "Jolly evening out there. Cold and crisp and all Kris Kingly. Has my aunty recovered sufficiently from the inspector's generous application of rubber hoses and heat lamps?"

"Miss Boisjoly is resting in her room, sir. She says that you may expect her for dinner."

"Not for cocktails?"

"Your aunt invites you to proceed at your chosen pace, sir."

"I'm way ahead of her, Puckeridge. They serve a mulled wine at the Sulky Cow that's decisively on the giggly side of the range between grog and laudanum."

"I'm gratified that you appreciated it. I myself have enjoyed the traditional Christmas wine at the Sulky Cow. "

"Yes, I understand you liven up the local from time to time," I said. "Tell me, between all the bare-knuckle brawling and dancing on tables, did you get a chance to take the measure of Major Fleming?"

"Yes, sir. Of late, the major was often at the pub when I was there. He was very generous with his anecdotes."

"Yes, I hear he wasn't shy about his accomplishments."

"Manifestly not, sir."

"You didn't see him there this morning, though."

"No, sir."

"Would it surprise you to learn that he bought a round of drinks for everyone?"

"Considerably, yes."

"And then said goodbye, forever."

"Indeed, sir?"

"So I'm told."

"One would think he knew that he was going to die."

"That," I said. "Or that he was already dead."

"Well-timed, Vickers," I said, entering the Heath Room to the welcome sight of my valet laying out my dinner togs next to a trolley of *eau de vie.* "I'll dress now, in fact. I've been sitting in a snowbank and, while I'm glad I did it and look forward to doing so again, I can tell you confidently that the time spent *between* sitting in snow banks is a dashed sight less comfortable." I began peeling away the damp layers. "So, what have we learned?"

"The inspector and Constable Kimble interviewed your aunt for nearly an hour," said Vickers, spreading a two-dimensional effigy of the young master on the bed while I assumed cocktail duty.

Vickers' drinks trolley is always fertile ground for scattershot serendipity and tonight's mixology prompt was a half-bottle of brandy, a pot of mustard, a pepper mill, and some clotted cream.

"Any idea what general direction the conversation took?" I asked while splashing two fingers of brandy into a teacup.

"The thrust of the discussion, as near as I could discern from the other side of the library door, was Miss Boisjoly's relationship with the deceased."

I glanced out the window for inspiration and found some. I threw up the sash and scooped a handful of snow into my brandy.

"Snow Toddy?"

"Thank you, no," demurred Vickers, holding my dinner trousers in approach formation. "I understand there will be Christmas drinks in the servants' hall this evening."

"I don't suppose you'd care to swap places, would you?" I said, stepping into my trousers. "I expect dinner with my aunt to be a singularly arcadian affair. Remind me to bring a long book."

"Mister Puckeridge wouldn't abide it, I'm afraid," said Vickers as he snapped braces onto my shoulders. "He's a man with a very lively sense of station."

"Oh yes? And quite comfortable in his own, I expect."

"Up to a point," said Vickers, addressing himself to the delicate matter of my collar stud. "If it's not taking a liberty, I'd venture that your aunt's diffident nature somewhat stifles Mister Puckeridge's domestic ambitions."

"Likes running a tight ship, does he?"

"There is that, sir." Vickers stepped back to survey the terrain. "But furthermore Mister Puckeridge gained his qualifications in some of the nation's more convivial great houses. I gather that the relatively insular social life of Herding House compares unfavourably."

"He's a big fish in a still pond, is he?"

"I fear he sees it that way, yes."

"Does that hamper your movements in any way?"

"Not at all, sir. As valet to a visiting gentleman, I'm afforded considerable latitude."

"And?"

"I'm afraid it's not good news," said Vickers, approaching

my bowtie like Degas approaching a promising lump of clay. "None of the staff can confirm Miss Boisjoly's movements at any time before our arrival this morning."

"And they've told Wittersham as much?"

"They have."

"Ah, well, that's roughly in line with expectations, at least." Now fully resplendent, I wandered to the window and looked out on the falling snow and the disappearing roof of Tannery Lodge. "In any case, there remain the footprints that Constable Kimble hopes to display to the court at Aunty Azalea's trial for murder. And I certainly fared no better at the Sulky Cow."

"The Sulky Cow?"

"The local. Social centre of town during the winter, it seems. I met four of the six regulars who claim to have been on hand for the final visitation this morning, reading from left to right, Sally Barnstable, landlady of the aforementioned Cow, Everett Trimble, Alderman, feed-store magnate, and Graze Hill's biggest fan, Trevor Barking, blacksmith and future child's toy tycoon, and town sponge Soaky Mike."

"I take it they confirmed the constable's contention that the major was alive this morning."

"They did. They also betrayed, in their turn, a peculiar reliance on the man. Miss Barnstable, for instance, made a point of expressing some resentment at the local hero using her establishment as a venue for self-promotion and free drinks, but it certainly sounds as though they had something of a symbiotic business relationship — the man could draw a crowd."

"Most intriguing, sir."

"I thought so. Then this Trimble chap, who presents himself as selfless civil servant but whom, I suspect, hopes to ride the swelling fame of Graze Hill to greater things, was rather relying on the major's reputation to grow that of the town." As I spoke I composed another cup of brandy and sill-snow. "You sure you won't have one of these?"

"Quite sure."

"Surprisingly good. Or maybe I just like brandy. Probably a bit of both. Anyhow, where was I? That's it, Trevor Barking. Some are born to blacksmithing, others have it thrust upon them. In Barking's case, as one who inherited a trade he doesn't fancy, it's both. He tells me that Flaps Fleming was going to finance his yo-yo factory. Do you know what a yo-yo is, Vickers?"

"I do not, sir, no."

"No, neither do I, but Barking seems quite confident that making them in a factory is the road to riches beyond the dreams of avarice. He tried to rope me into investing."

"I trust you were able to resist temptation."

"By a hair. He paints a very compelling picture, our Mister Barking. And finally there's Soaky Mike, who appears to have made an industry out of begging drinks off regulars of the Sulky Cow, and is only prevented from becoming fabulously wealthy in this pursuit by Miss Barnstable, who limits his intake to some specific frequency."

"Do we presume that Mister Soaky Mike had some dependency on the deceased?"

"Not as such, no. In fact I'd say that they were largely in competition for the same market. He did, however, say something quite grave and cryptic before staggering off into

66

the night — he said that the major was no hero."

"Perhaps he just meant to himself, personally."

"I suppose that's a possibility, but he delivered it with a strength of feeling that rather transcended the rancour that would naturally occur between rivals for the increasingly scarce charity round."

"Did I understand you to say that there remained two outstanding members of this gallery of local personalities?"

"You did," I confirmed. "Apparently Flaps Fleming had family in town — chap named Cosmo Millicent is the major's nephew, but staying with the vicar, which on its own makes him a curiosity, in my view. Finally, there remains a sixth member of the cast of the Sulky Cow, made all the more mysterious by the fact that he's a recent arrival — also a guest of the Reverend Padget — and nobody knows his name."

"Did he not give it, sir?" asked Vickers, who hated to see a convention, however small, flouted.

"No, he did. His name's just too long to recall. This is a small town, you understand."

"Of course."

"I expect we'll see them at church tonight. Among very few others. I understand that Graze Hill is something of a ghost town over Christmas."

"So I have been informed by the household staff."

I chewed on the last of my brandy slush and once again looked longingly out at the smooth snowdrifts slowly forming around the trees.

"I suppose I should be joining Aunty Azalea for the Christmas binge. Incidentally, Vickers, you don't know where one could lay one's hands on a full set of the war diaries of Charles à Court Repington by any chance, do you?"

"I'm afraid not."

"I thought not. It was a nine-to-one longshot, at best. For some reason the killer chucked volume one on the fire at the scene of the crime."

"Most curious."

"And if volume two is anything to go by, volume one is a bit of a brick — it'll take some time to determine its significance in the death of Major Fleming."

"Indeed, sir," agreed Vickers. "Volume one is six hundred and twenty-one pages."

"Have you read it, Vickers?"

"Yes, sir."

"That's unexpectedly handy. What's it about, in broad strokes?"

"As you have no doubt surmised, the volumes constitute the personal reminiscences of the war correspondent Charles à Court Repington. They largely recount his meetings with influential personalities of the day, such as General Petain and Lord Kitchener."

"You remember all that, do you?"

"Vividly."

"Without looking, Vickers, are you wearing gloves or not?"

"I don't recall."

"Extraordinary. Well, out with it then, what does volume one of Charles à Court Repington's memoirs of the war tell us about aeronautic battles in general or, ideally, Major Aaron Fleming in particular?"

"Absolutely nothing, sir."

"Merry Christmas, all," I called out to the long, oak dining hall which, apart from Aunty Azalea at the head of a table with room for twenty, was empty. "How are we going to pull the Christmas crackers if I'm sat all the way at this end?"

The table was elaborately set for two over a bright red table-cloth with a green, lace runner from one end to the other. A wildfire crackled in an oversized fireplace which occupied much of the interior wall. The exterior wall gave onto the opposite side of the house from my room, and its large windows framed the mood-setting scene of white-coated pine trees on the hill and a dense fall of pudgy snowflakes. Aunty Boisjoly was wearing a sort of flowered number, and she'd allowed her lady's maid to take some original tack with her hair.

"I can't bear the bang of Christmas crackers, Anty," she said as I planted the Christmas kiss on the proffered cheek, "but in the spirit of the season I had Puckeridge cut some open. He'll bring them with the port."

"Jolly good. Perhaps we can get him to run the goose through a meat grinder and whirl the peas into a fine paste."

"Oh, Anty, don't be tiresome. I've had an appalling day."

"Of course. Sorry. I understand Inspector Wittersham's scrutiny went into extra innings."

"He just kept asking the same questions, phrased ever so subtly differently."

"He was trying to catch you out," I said and then, "Yes, please, Puckeridge, to the rim," as Puckeridge had just entered armed with a bottle of Moët & Chandon '26. He was followed by the kitchen maid outfitted with a silver soup tureen.

"I regret to tell you, Aunty, that Inspector Wittersham has you at the very top of his naughty list," I continued but was immediately shot down by old-school snobbery.

"Please, Anty." Aunty Azalea frowned and pointed hard at the help with her eyes from beneath a hooded brow.

"I'm quite confident that Puckeridge and... what's the girl's name, Puckeridge?"

"Alice, sir," said Puckeridge. The girl, a short but robust, chipper sort of kitchen maid, smiled and curtsied at the recognition, and then set about ladling out the consommé.

"I'm quite confident that Puckeridge and Alice are as aware of the facts as we are, if not more so, aren't you, Puckeridge?"

"I couldn't possibly say, sir," replied the butler, and then popped the cork of the champagne. "May I pour, sir?"

"Please do. What's more, Aunty, such is Puckeridge's strict sense of duty, he's literally deaf to anything said in the household that doesn't directly concern its operation. Isn't that so, Puckeridge?"

"I beg your pardon, sir — I wasn't listening."

"There you go. Cheers to you, Aunty Azalea," I raised my glass. "I wish upon you a Christmas of new beginnings and an end to sad tidings."

"Merry Christmas, Anty." Aunty raised her glass. The flickering light from the fire reflected in it and glistened in her eyes. Puckeridge and Alice discreetly withdrew.

"There, there, Aunty," I said. "I'm not going to let

Inspector Wittersham simplify his life by railroading you for murder. I've foiled his dark designs before, you know."

Aunty put down her glass and looked into it, or at any rate she looked down. "It's not always about you, Anthony."

I had the momentary and novel sensation of speechlessness. I filled the unfamiliar space with an appreciation of an excellent year for champagne — nearly as good as the '24 and a wholesale improvement over the regrettable '25.

"I'm sorry, Aunty," I said, with the cold epiphany of one catching oneself comparing vintage years when one might have been reflecting on why one's maiden aunt was crying at the Christmas table. "Of course you're right. Were you and Flaps very close?"

"You sound like the inspector."

"No need to resort to insults, Aunty," I said. "I'm sorry you've lost your friend."

"He was more than that, Anthony."

For the second time in the span of a minute I was at a loss for words. I was overwhelmed by the stark pathos of the situation — had Aunty Azalea found love late in life only to have it snatched away so brutally?

"I didn't realise. How long...?"

"Oh, don't be ridiculous, Anty. It wasn't like that. I just mean that Flaps was very dear to me. He understood me — and I understood him — as unlike anyone I've ever known."

Aunty Azalea stood then and brought her champagne to the fireplace. I joined her and together we cast melancholy thoughts into the flames, where they burned brightly. It was just the sort of fireplace you want for the incineration of melancholy — composed of rough stone, as high as a fully-grown Graze Hill Golden and wide enough to accommodate wrought-iron racks on either side, stacked with frozen logs until they'd defrosted enough to burn. Very practical and very jolly.

"Tell me about him," I said.

"He liked to be alone. We had that in common." Aunty Azalea looked into her champagne glass, as though just that moment realising that she had it with her. Then in a single throw she swallowed it all. "I say, that's quite good, isn't it?"

"I'll get you another." I retrieved the bottle and topped up our glasses.

"And he was a hero, Anty. He would tell me his adventures — he was shot down over the channel, you know. It's how he lost his eye. He would tell me about the war and it was as though I was there. He took me with him, metaphorically. I flew in a plane, Anty, over Belgium and over France and Germany. He was a very vivid storyteller."

"So I understand," I said. "Did he never suggest going to the Sulky Cow?"

Aunty shook her head firmly. "He understood me, Anty, that's what you're missing. He knew that I wouldn't have wanted to hear about a *public* house."

"I heard that he was beginning to warm to the society of strangers."

"He was," confirmed Aunty with a nod. "He said he wanted to face the world again, that I was giving him the strength to do so, and that we should do it together."

"And how did you respond to that?"

"I couldn't possibly, Anty. I'd have sooner died."

"I see," I said. "You didn't happen to share that view with Inspector Wittersham, did you?"

"Of course, Anty. Why shouldn't I?"

CHAPTER SEVEN

The Strange Scene on Saint Stephen's Steeple Seen

There was more champagne, and smoked salmon with shallots, a '24 *Chateau Meursault* Pinot Noir, roast duck and baked potatoes, and many tears before the plum pudding was set on fire.

I put a handsome effort into talking Aunty Azalea into coming to church, made all the more valiant by the fact that I was, in reality, hoping that she would talk me out of it. In the end, heavy with goose fat and burgundy and hence slow and defenceless against natural predators, I elected to extend my walk to the church and simultaneously reconnoitre the path between Tannery Lodge and the Sulky Cow.

The fresh layer of snow had reduced the major's tracks to shallow indentations, but unless a Grizzly Bear had been through the woods recently, the footprints left by Constable Kimble were clear and easily followed. Presently, I was atop the hill, looking down onto the sleepy, snowy village of Graze Hill. I looked back at Tannery Lodge and in a moment realised that the distance over the hill was, unsurprisingly, now I think of it, shorter than going around. I continued down the hill, keeping pace with the constable's tracks, and in minutes I was at the now darkened Sulky Cow. The road meandered pastorally from that point and curved to the left, where it met the doors of the church, and then ambled away toward the remaining houses. The effect was to make of the church a storybook, snow-capped centrepiece.

Saint Stephen's was of the sweetly modest species of village chapel, with walls of plastered rubble, carved stone ornamentals, steep, copper-tiled roofs, and a high clock tower with pointed belfry. Approaching from the Sulky Cow, all roads appeared to lead to the front of the church, and to the rest of the village it presented an amiable profile, with stained-glass windows that glowed from within. There was a handsome clock face on all four sides of the tower and the belfry was splendidly detailed, but what really drew the eye, the touch that set the whole thing off, the splash of wine on the communion dress, was a gleaming golden cow weather vane.

It was a likeness of Hildy, with scale-model pins that rendered her, seen from below, not unlike the original three-valve Bugatti racing car, and under a full winter moon it glimmered in a regrettably unmissable manner. Few, if any, would be able to visit the metropolitan centre of Graze Hill and later credibly claim 'Weather vane? What weather vane?', though that would clearly be the merciful thing to do.

Presently the doors of the church opened and what appeared to be a man dressed as a birthday cake stepped out onto the top step. I took this to be Vicar Padget, who apparently went in for the High Anglican fashion of purple vestments for Eucharist.

"Welcome, welcome," said Padget, with the deliberate sort of austerity of men who deliver bad news professionally. "Welcome to Saint Stephen's." He was a short and slight man, and he wore a cope of purple velvet and ivory piping that had been made for a bigger vicar. He completed the picture of the oppressed, harried village parson with fingers that fidgeted as though knitting an intricate and invisible cardigan.

"Good evening, Father Padget. I'm Anthony Boisjoly, nephew to Azalea Boisjoly."

"I know, Mister Boisjoly." Padget smiled sympathetically and shook my hand. Then he looked searchingly behind me over thick, round glasses that had steamed to an opaque finish in the cold air. "I had hoped to see your poor aunt this evening."

"She wasn't up to it. She told me to have an extra helping on her behalf."

"Oh, very well. I..."

"Lovely church, Saint Stephen's."

"Yes, yes." The vicar looked into the glowing interior with a dubious accord. "I'm afraid it's a little cold — we don't have a coal stove, as such." He smiled weakly. I smiled weakly back, and we were in unvoiced but perfect alignment on the gravity of the absence of coal-heating in church. "And the roof leaks, when it rains. And sometimes when it's not raining, strangely enough."

I was sufficiently habituated to the practises of the country vicar that I had come to expect this appeal, and I was about to ask Padget if the collection plate would trust my personal cheque, but he hadn't finished the inventory of woe.

"Be careful where you sit, incidentally, many of the pews

are cracked and it's not unheard of for parishioners to receive a nasty splinter."

"Noted."

"And there are termites."

"The clocktower is very practical," I suggested as a panacea. Padget looked upward, either at the clock in question or toward a vengeful God.

"It's never worked properly. It wants manual winding by hand-crank. Separately, you understand — north, east, west and south."

"One of Mister Trimble's initiatives?" I asked.

"Possibly not the most effective use of discretionary funds," said Padget with that indulgent smile that's on the final exam at vicar school.

"At least you have a very nice weather vane."

A cloud passed over the clergyman's face.

"Yes," he said, staring into the middle field. "There is that." He appeared to mentally leave me for a moment, and when he returned he brought along a change of subject. "Tell me, Mister Boisjoly, how is your dear aunt coping with the tragic news?"

"About as well as one might expect, under the circumstances," I said. "And considering those circumstances are the brutal murder of her only friend on Christmas morning."

"Oh dear."

"Yes. Did you know the major?"

"Oh yes, yes. Yes indeed." The vicar nodded earnestly, as though shooing away any doubt. "I was ministering to him.

I'd like to think that in some small way I contributed to his decision to..." Padget sought inspiration from above, "...resume his place in society."

"He was coming to church?"

"Every Sunday, of late. He was growing quite enthusiastic about it, in fact."

"And he was frequenting the Sulky Cow."

"So I understand. Mister Barking tells me that the major was quite the famous raconteur," said Padget with the forbearance of the long-suffering shepherd for the errant lamb.

There was a square-hole-round-peggish feel about something the vicar had said, and I was struggling to put my finger on it when Barking appeared from the interior of the church, wearing a verger's cassock. He said, "Evening, Mister Boisjoly," then took a firm hold of the bell-pull and gave it a good, hard, yank. A portentous 'ding' rang out overhead, followed by a deep, rich peal that waved over the silent night as only a church bell can. Barking appeared to derive much catharsis from the act, as though it settled some long-running disagreement he'd been having with the bell. He nodded resolutely and faded back into the interior of the church.

"Industrious chap, your verger," I observed. "I'm surprised he can spare the time for much vergering."

"He's a tremendous help in the evenings. And, of course..." The vicar once again raised his eyes skyward for strength. "...he made the weather vane."

"Modelled on the work of his father, I'm told. Mister Trimble suggested I have a look at the museum. I understand it's fashioned along the lines of the Royal Albert, but with the nuance of the Louvre."

"Mister Trimble subscribes to the grand vision school of municipal planning — he believes that if Graze Hill acts like a boomtown, it will become one."

"I understand he was putting a lot of stock into the prominence of the local hero."

"Such a pity." Padget twined his fingers and studied them carefully. "Mister Trimble was very fond of the major — we all were, of course — but his father, Sergeant Morris Trimble, served with him. Owed Major Fleming his life."

"Odd he didn't mention that."

"He will. Mister Trimble has a disarmingly erratic speaking style, but he gets around to most things, eventually. Ah!" Padget exclaimed at someone behind me, and I turned to take in what, at first glance, appeared to be one half of a Pat and Mike cross-talk act. He was a handsome young chap, perhaps my age, with clean-cut aquiline features that seemed designed for reduced wind resistance. He wore a white overcoat on top of a deafening red and black chequered boat jacket which, in turn, was performing the public service of covering an emerald green waistcoat. He had a monocle in his left eye, which was fortunate because if he hadn't had a monocle he'd have needed one to complete the effect of having been dressed as a last-minute replacement for master of ceremonies of a Vaudeville performing animal act.

"Mister Millicent, how *are* you holding up?" Padget grasped the young man's outstretched hand in both of his and cocked his head like a puppy with a conundrum.

"Oh, all right, all things and all that, what?" said Mister Millicent with a lisp that spoke of public schools and fox hunts and a worryingly uncomplicated family tree.

"Mister Boisjoly, this is Cosmo Millicent," said Padget. Then he lowered his voice theatrically, as though navigating the audience through a tricky plot development. "Mister Millicent is Major Fleming's nephew."

"I'm very sorry about your uncle, Mister Millicent," I said.

"Oh, quite. Thanks very... Cosmo, though, shall we say?"

"Pleasure Cosmo. Call me Anthony or, if you're pressed for time, Anty."

"Right ho, Anty."

"Shall we tour the museum?" I suggested. "And leave the vicar to gather his flock?"

Cosmo and I wandered into the little church.

"I understand that you're staying with Mister Padget while in Graze Hill," I said.

"Yes. Not my very first choice, if I'm completely honest, but there's not a broad selection. It was that or a boarding house in Steeple Herding that smelled rather of barn, and I would have been expected to either help with the milking or transcribe the life story of the family patriarch, whose chief claim to notoriety is that he's never been further than Stevenage."

"I'd have been sorely tempted."

"The vicarage is closer to my uncle."

"Your uncle's place is even closer. Couldn't you have stayed with him?"

"I could have done, yes," said Cosmo, tentatively. "He asked me, of course, and it pained me to say no, but have you seen Tannery Lodge? It's not really the sort of space two grown men could comfortably share."

"I have seen it, and I take your meaning. You visited him there, then?"

Cosmo nodded. "Regularly. We were negotiating terms, as it were."

"Terms?"

"His life story, don't you know, what?" said Cosmo. We had entered the northern transept and were confronted by a tin likeness of Hildy. She stood, somewhat self-consciously for a tin statue, on a card table which was draped with purple cloth to form an honorary plinth. "Did you notice the gold version of that thing on the tower? There's a real one, too, you know. It's a most extraordinary animal. Four feet tall if it's an inch."

"We've met. Only briefly but I feel I'm a better man for it and, I flatter myself to think, she, too, remembers the occasion fondly." I wandered the little museum of Graze Hill artefacts, including a series of elaborate cassocks behind glass vitrines and an astonishingly large collection of bovine photography. "So you and your uncle had not yet settled terms with regards to his biography?"

"In the main we had. A few fiddly bits remained, some 'i's in want of dots, 't's short a few crosses, but he'd agreed in principle to let me write the thing."

"You're a professional writer?"

"Ah, well, in the strictest sense of the word 'professional', no, I'm not. Not yet, at any rate. But what is writing, at the end of the day, what? It's just bunging the vitals down on paper and a working knowledge of the thesaurus to keep you using the word 'temerity' twice in the same sentence."

"You certainly *sound* like a professional writer," I

observed. "Will the story be published posthumously?"

"It'll rather have to be, now, won't it?"

"Manifestly so, yes. But how will you determine the aforementioned vitals without benefit of the horse's mouth?"

"The very point that has been much on my mind, as it happens," said Cosmo meditatively. "I don't know."

"Surely you kept detailed notes from your evenings at Tannery Lodge and the Sulky Cow."

"Oh, quite. Reams and reams. Yes, indeed." Cosmo briefly perked up at the recollection. "I was rather counting on the old man's help to sort through it all, mind you. Provide a bit of what we in the writing game call 'background', don't you know?"

"Ah, there you are, Millicent." The rafters of Saint Stephen's quivered existentially with this booming announcement. Cosmo and I turned to receive what I took to be a baritone soloist appearing in the role of a country squire. He was twenty-odd years older than Cosmo and I and he had that bushy, jowly appearance of a class of gentleman who grow bushy and jowly as a matter of duty to God and country. He cultivated a grey moustache that passed beneath his nose as part of a full orbit around his head, taking in mutton-chop sideburns and the coastal region of a glistening bald pate. He was dressed in tweed and yet somehow managed to wear it like a military uniform. Time had broadened the foundation and polished the dome, but I recognised this as the modern manifestation of the smiling young man standing to the left of Flaps Fleming in the squadron portrait.

"Hello Monty," said Cosmo. "Anty — Mister Boisjoly — this is Flight-Lieutenant Montgomery Hern-Fowler, RAF."

"Boisjoly, you say?" bellowed Monty. "Knew a Boisjoly at Whitehall during the war. Edward or some such."

"Edmond, I expect," I said. "My father. He managed to find his niche in Army Intelligence."

"Perhaps not, then. Chap I'm thinking of spent all his time drinking in the VIP mess."

"That was him," I confirmed. "'They also serve, those who only stand drinks,' he used to say. His speciality was rapid-response hospitality and precision bombing, so to speak. He claimed to have invented the Five Inch Field Gun — three parts gin, two parts champagne, poured gently over cracked ice. He said it came to him one day as a matter of necessity when an entire shipment of seltzer was delivered flat."

"I did indeed know your father," said Monty, very much in the manner of one turning a page on a sordid chapter of the past. "What the devil is that?"

"A cow," I explained with reference to the tin likeness of Hildy.

"Looks like one of those ridiculous dogs. Sausage-shaped German mutts."

"Dachshund."

"Bless you."

"I take it this is your first visit to Saint Stephen's, Monty."

"Blew in last week."

"And what brings you to Graze Hill?"

"Looking up old brothers in arms. I came to visit my old wingman, Flaps Fleming."

"What unfortunate timing," I said. "You have my sympathies."

"Poor chap," Monty solemnly yelled. "Knife in the back, they tell me."

"A very literal way to go," I confirmed. "I understand you were among those present when he made his farewell tour of the nation's pubs."

"I was."

"Then tell me something, gentlemen," I addressed myself to Cosmo and Monty, "are you quite certain of the time that the major was in the pub?"

"Oh, absolutely," said Cosmo. "From about ten till just around eleven. Quite sure."

"That barmaid kept pointing at the clock," added Monty. "Kept that poor sot — Soapy Mike — on some sort of schedule."

"Soaky Mike," I corrected gently. "And when the major left you, was there anything unusual in his departure?"

"There rather was, now you mention it," answered Cosmo. "He wished me luck... with the book, you know... with a sort of, oh, I don't know..." Cosmo squinted and doubtless wished he'd thought to bring his thesaurus to church. "...finality?"

"I see. Monty?"

"Not that I noticed," shouted Monty thoughtfully. "Why do you ask?".

"Just sticking my nose in," I explained. "For the moment the chief suspect is my maiden aunt and one feels a certain duty, you know, when one's flesh and blood is looking at a noose from the wrong side of the blindfold."

"Does you credit, young man," whooped Monty with feeling.

"Thank you."

"Unless she did it. She didn't do it, did she?"

"Certainly not. It just happens that there's a — so far — unexplained sequence of events that require either my aunt to be a calculating and cold-blooded killer or Major Aaron Fleming to have visited the Sulky Cow three hours after his death."

"Probably a ghost." Monty barked this with a calm sincerity that caught me off guard.

"Do you believe in ghosts, Monty?"

"Of course. Seen some. During the war. Flaps saw them too, as it happens."

Before I could give voice to some variation of "Wha'?", Barking whooshed into the little museum in a flurry of worn silk and said, "If you'd care to take a pew, gentlemen."

While we'd been nattering the rest of the congregation had arrived and the church was now teeming with as many as eight parishioners, not counting the vicar. Barking toured the premises, gently swinging a tin thurible and trailing thin strains of incense. Saint Stephen's, as I had guessed when I saw Padget dressed in mauve and mad abandon, was a High Church holdout in dairy country, where few had time to spare for church at Christmas.

I settled in next to Ivor and behind Sally Barnstable and Soaky Mike, one of whom sat in the first row, no doubt, to gain early access to the Communion wine and the other, with equally little doubt, to stop him. Cosmo, Monty, and Everett found comparatively splinter-free surfaces on the other side of the aisle.

In light of the day's events Padget must have struggled

before settling on the *Sermon on the Mount* from the Book of Matthew which, among its generous list of benedictions, blesses those who mourn. He balanced that out in the second reading with a crowd favourite from the Book of Wisdom, including the hit "The souls of the just are in the hand of God, and no torment shall touch them." The vicar leaned into that one a bit, eyeing the absent choir longingly, as he came dangerously close to singing the reading himself before he remembered that he was in an English church and not some hot-blooded, Italian cathedral, and composed himself.

"Peace be with you, Inspector," I said when passing the peace. "Have there been any developments?"

"And on you, Mister Boisjoly. I'm afraid so. It would appear that Constable Kimble was right about a romantic relationship between your aunt and Major Fleming."

"And peace be upon Constable Kimble, though he's a dimwit. My aunt has assured me that her feelings toward the major were the cordial sentiments of good neighbours."

Ivor shook his head as one does when an inveterate gambler tells you he's onto a sure thing, and Padget began his homily, which turned out to be an account of a Christmas Day he spent in the trenches.

The hymns were short and popular and hence well-chosen for a sparse congregation with limited rehearsal time. I don't object to it but I mention for the record that I was rather carrying Ivor, who had a tendency to hide what I'm sure was a rich baritone beneath a drone of half-remembered lyrics to some carol unknown to all but himself.

The eucharist was quickly dispensed with and, as is customary after such affairs, there was a clamouring for the door. I was anxious to pick up my conversation with Monty at roughly the point where he had said "ghost" but Padget was running defence at the exit. I issued him a perfunctory "lovely sermon, Father" but he wouldn't let go of my hand, instead drawing me into a zone of confidence.

"I say, Mister Boisjoly, you wouldn't help me out with something, would you?" he said in a tone of spirited conspiracy.

"Of course Vicar. Give it a name and I'll give it cracking good try."

"I understand you read Classics at Oxford."

"It was that or law," I replied. "But that carried the very real risk of leaving school with professional qualifications."

"I wonder if you might give me your opinion on something..." Padget slipped a folded length of heavy notepaper from his hymn book. "...Just a modest work of my own. I'd be very pleased to have your honest views."

"Absolute pleasure, Vic," I said, entrusting the paper to my inside pocket.

"I seek the unvarnished truth, you understand. No need to spare my feelings."

"I'll have you crying like a schoolgirl, Father, you have my word on it."

"Oh, uh, quite. Well, thank you, Mister Boisjoly."

I moved to intercept Monty as he and Cosmo were absorbed by the snowy night, but Ivor drew me back with a compelling inquiry: "Did Mister Padget tell you, Mister Boisjoly?"

"He may well have," I replied austerely. There was something worryingly self-satisfied in Ivor's tone. "The vicar and I share many confidences and a wide range of interests."

"I'm referring to recent revelations regarding your aunt and Major Fleming."

"Have there been such revelations?"

Padget and Ivor shared an uncomfortable moment.

"Why, yes," said Padget. "Did you not know?"

"Possibly. It depends almost entirely on what we're talking about."

"Miss Boisjoly and the major were to be married. I had been calling upon them at Tannery Lodge to discuss a high church ceremony."

Ivor, to his credit, strained every muscle in his face in an effort to appear sympathetic.

"That hardly proves that she killed him, Inspector," I said. "If anything, it makes it less likely."

"That isn't all of it, Mister Boisjoly."

"Very well, what is all of it?"

"I regret to say, Mister Boisjoly," said Padget, "that the major intended to break off the engagement."

CHAPTER EIGHT

Hildy Discovers Her Hidden Depths

"I don't object to you persecuting my aunt, you understand, Inspector."

Ivor and I were walking in the direction of the hill, he to continue to Constable Kimble's cosy little constable cottage on the border of Steeple Herding, and I to return to the house of my aunt. The night was cold and still, and the snow had ceased falling.

"It's all part of the game, of course." I continued my theme. "You focus the combined energies of the forces of the state on establishing a case against a single helpless old woman, while I doggedly pursue the real killer. These are the ground rules and I accept them." I cast a sideways eye at the inspector to see if he was picking up on my subtle ironies. He was lighting his pipe. "I just think you might make a show of actually investigating the crime. Couldn't do you any harm, you know. Gets you out and about, you'll meet new people. You never know, Inspector, if you broaden your horizons you might find any number of people to railroad for a crime they couldn't possibly have committed."

"Are you quite finished, Mister Boisjoly?"

"I think you know me better than that. Have you spoken to Cosmo Millicent?"

"The major's nephew? Yes, we spoke to him this afternoon."

"Then you know that he was counting on the hero's blessing to write a tell-all biography."

"We do."

"Well, what if the major denied said blessing?" I asked. "What if the major dismissed the project, and then went on to disparage Cosmo's vocabulary and his approach to omniscient voice? He strikes me as the sensitive sort of poet."

"By all accounts the major was cooperating with the book," said Ivor between puffs on his pipe.

"And this Montgomery Hern-Fowler cove. He breezes into town and a few days later his old army buddy is dead with a knife in his back," I observed. "Plainly metaphorical, to my mind. Perhaps the Flight-Lieutenant was resentful of the major's celebrity. I can see it as though it was playing out right there on that snowdrift — a line of brave boys, shivering in a dark, wet, trench, as the first grey glow of dawn outlines the horizon. An ominous hush descends. Then the major gives the order to go over the top and drawn, as these young men are, from the cannon-fodder class, over they go. Flashes of blinding light, ricochets of flying shrapnel, chaos and fury, young lives wasted in a single charge, and the hill is taken. Then the major steps up and plants the flag and declares the battle won, and he's in all the papers back home and gets a letter from the king. You can see how that sort of thing would engender bitter feelings."

"The major was Hern-Fowler's wingman," pointed out Ivor. "They only ever saw a trench from five thousand feet."

"The principle stands. In any case, I'm just getting started. Everett Trimble. Did you speak to him?"

"Most decidedly so."

"Memorable encounter, isn't he?" I said. "Rather like stepping out of a calm reverie and into traffic in Piccadilly Circus. Did you know that his father served with Flaps?"

We had arrived at the crossroads and stopped there in the stillness. We looked back on the little, snow-coddled village. Ivor drew luxuriously on his pipe.

"He mentioned it. Claims the major saved his life."

"I heard that. Did he say how?"

"Indeed he did," said Ivor. "Couldn't have stopped him if I'd tried — turns out the major never mentioned it and it was Hern-Fowler told him that it was Fleming that noticed Sargeant Trimble's poor depth perception, and made him chief mechanic so that he wouldn't have to fly."

"Is that all?" I asked. "When I learned that Everett's father owed the major his life, I naturally assumed that there would have been more drama — shells bursting overhead as, his own body riddled with bullets and shrapnel, he carries his wounded brother through the smoke and mire of no-man's land, breathing a hoarse vow through clenched teeth, 'Not this time, Jerry. Not this time.'"

"No, the major merely gave him a comfortable ground assignment. If it's drama you want, though, Sergeant Trimble was killed in a chance encounter with a propeller at RAF

Acklington toward the end of the war."

"How darkly ironic," I observed. "Perhaps Everett's motive has a more recent origin, then. Did you know that he was mounting a national-scale public relations campaign to raise the profile of the town of Graze Hill, the foundation of which was the fame of Major Fleming?"

"Of course. There's meant to be a bronze statue erected right there." Ivor pointed with his pipe at the town square formed where the road angled before the church. The golden cow glistened hideously in the moonlight. "Hardly a motive for murder. Quite the opposite I'd have said."

"I understand the unveiling is being pushed forward," I said. "Could it be that the famously publicity-shy major was unwilling to participate in the crass exploitation of his reputation?"

Ivor removed his pipe from his lips to allow them to shrug noncommittally. "It's generally understood that the major was finally coming to terms with his fame. He was frequenting the Sulky Cow, attending church, keeping company with your aunt..."

"Talking of the pub, what do you make of Sally-Ann Barnstable?" I asked with adroit deflection. "She affects to have resented the major's Saturday matinées, but what sort of pub landlady objects to crowds of thirsty revellers?"

"The sort who isn't a landlady at all, I'd venture," said Ivor, smoking and gazing upon Graze Hill like a man about to tell a wry punchline. "It's not her pub, after all."

"Isn't it?" I asked. "Everyone seems to think it is. Whose pub is it?"

"Miss Barnstable is broadly referred to as the landlady

because in practice she functions as such, but the Sulky Cow belongs to her father, one Mister Michael Barnstable."

"Michael? Do you mean to say that Soaky Mike is the proprietor of the Sulky Cow? And Sally's father?"

"He is."

"Blimey. No wonder she keeps such a warder's eye on him — he'd drink all the profits in a single sitting."

"I daresay he would."

"You've met him then," I said. "Did you gather that Soaky Mike is among the few who have a natural immunity to the charms of Flaps Fleming?"

"If you're referring to Mister Barnstable's stated belief that the major wasn't the hero he claimed to be, I don't think there's much to it."

"These things often run deep, Inspector. I once knew a boy at Eton who was unrepentant in his seditious views of Prime Minister Asquith. Turns out that he had cause — his allowance had been stopped for proposing to the downstairs maid something he'd read in a poem by D.H. Lawrence."

Ivor regarded me as though trying to recall what particular species of rare bird I was.

"You went to school with Lord Asquith's son?"

"He was only Prime Minister Asquith at the time."

"Nevertheless," resigned Ivor. "Mister Barnstable contends that the major couldn't have piloted a plane with only one eye, because he wouldn't have been able to see the stick shift."

"But... the major lost his eye in battle. Air battle."

"Precisely," confirmed Ivor. "And aeroplanes don't have

gearboxes. You see why I didn't take 'Soaky Mike' very seriously."

"I do," I confessed. "That still leaves us the mysterious Trevor Barking — blacksmith, industrialist, inventor, sculptor, reluctant yet admirably competent church layman. He's a dark horse, that one."

"What about him?"

"You don't know?"

"Probably," said Ivor. "You see, Mister Boisjoly, what you amateur enthusiasts fail to understand is that most police work is dull, repetitive, rote. Asking questions, noting the answers, moving on. Mister Barking has been thoroughly interviewed."

"Ah, well, then. You'll already know about the yo-yo syndicate."

We shared a moment of calm reflection, then, listening to the creak and crackle of the woods, and breathing in the cool, crisp air lightly scented with the smoke of coal and wood and pipe tobacco.

"The what?" asked Ivor, finally.

"Mister Barking was relying on the major to back his British yo-yo franchise."

"What is a yo-yo? And why would it need to be franchised?"

"It's a child's toy," I explained. "Apparently they're the leopard's loungewear in America, and Barking has a plan to corner the UK market. All he needs is ten thousand pounds of what he calls 'working capital'."

"And the major gave it to him?"

"The major was playing his cards close to his chest,

according to Barking," I explained. "He was giving him five thousand pounds up front, with a further five thousand to follow as production kicked into gear."

"So you're saying Barking was running some sort of fiddle, and when the major wanted to know how his money was being spent, Barking killed him."

"Well, no," I said. "In fact, it would appear that Barking had yet to receive the first instalment. He tried to touch me for it, in fact. That's how I learned of the enterprise."

"That sounds like the opposite of motive to me, Mister Boisjoly," said Ivor. "Indeed, of all the spinsters, bachelors, and gin-soaked widowers that the season has marooned in Graze Hill, the only one who wasn't in some fashion indebted to the major is your aunt. Even Mister Padget was counting on a significant donation to do up the church."

"Must have been a very significant donation indeed. I happened to cast my eyes upward during *Lo! He Comes With Clouds Descending* and I could clearly make out Ursa Minor through a substantial hole in the roof."

"I noticed that."

"And yet there are disbursements for four-way clocks and, of all things, golden calves on the belfry," I said.

Ivor and I were once again musing on the glittering monstrosity on top of the church when there came to us a most unexpected sound...

"Moo?"

We shared a curious glance and then proceeded along the path formed of sleigh-tracks until we were almost in sight of Herding House. There, embedded in a snowbank up to her briskets, was Hildy the midget cow. By all appearances, she had been drawn by urgent business on the other side of the hill and was heading that way when her little legs proved unequal to the task.

"How the devil did that happen?" asked Ivor.

"Careful breeding," I explained. "That, Inspector, is a best-in-show specimen of the Graze Hill Golden. Unique to the region. Notice the slightly elongated yet proportional back, the broad, foreshortened neck, the copper-toned pelt and matey expression. Note also that the snowbank in which she finds herself stuck is little more than a foot deep."

Hildy looked at us with a doleful expression of wounded pride, and spoke a plaintive "moo" that conveyed in a syllable, "If you're going to laugh then go ahead and get on with it."

"What do we do?" asked Ivor, with that disarming tone of those who find themselves out of their depth, and assume that others do not.

"Will Constable Kimble be in?" I asked. "You could pop over and bring him back. I imagine he could sling a medium-sized cow over his shoulder. I'll keep Hildy company."

"I think not."

"I think I should. We have a bond."

"I mean that I have no intention of walking fifteen minutes to the police cottage and back in aid of a stranded cow."

Further debate was rendered academic by crunching footsteps heralding the arrival of the keeper of the Sulky Cow.

"What are you doing with my cow?" demanded Sally with that air of easy authority God grants innkeepers and traffic magistrates.

"Good evening, Sally," I said. "At the moment we're doing what we can to comfort the poor creature. She's stuck in the snow."

"I can see that," said Sally, hands on her hips and fire in her eye. "What I want to know is how it happened."

"Ah, there you take us into uncharted territory. It's never my practice to evade responsibility but my hands, in this rare case, are clean. She was like that when we got here."

Sally shook her head in dismay and disappointment.

"There's a shovel in the little barn behind the pub," she said.

"I'll make keen note of it," I said, momentarily baffled, but then Sally glared at me beneath hooded eyes, and I saw the light. "Ah. I'll just go and fetch it, shall I?"

I skidded and slipped back down the hill to the manger. While there I noted that Hildy's confinement was enforced with a simple stile — in effect, she had been on her honour to remain under house arrest but, pining for my company, had tracked me like a leopard until meeting her match in a fourteen-inch snowdrift. I collected the shovel and used it as a walking stick to scamper back to the scene of the emergency. In the perhaps five minutes I had been gone, I felt, there had occurred a palpable change in the general attitude toward Boisjolys. Sally had positioned herself in front of Hildy, offering spiritual comfort in the form of a familiar face and, I expect, performing a forensic examination of Hildy's breath.

"Mister Boisjoly, what did you do with the remains of the mulled wine?"

I smiled limply.

97

"Before we address that, Miss Barnstable, I can tell you that one thing I didn't do with it is allow it to fall into the hands of Soaky Mike. I knew that you would disapprove."

"You fed my cow mulled wine?"

"It was heavily diluted with snow. There was an incident."

Ivor assumed the distance and disposition of a bystander, and smiled happily at the ad-hoc nativity.

"Casting a detective's eye over the scene of the crime," he observed with the flat, academic detachment of one who can refer to a cow stuck in a snowbank as a crime scene, "I would say that the cow, having tasted the wine and found it pleasing, was induced to seek a second helping. She must have endeavoured to follow Mister Boisjoly. The poor animal's probably been trapped here for hours."

"Thank you, Inspector," I said with theatrical irony, then turning to Sally, "I'll just dig her out, shall I?"

Sally replied with a very eloquent crossing of the arms and lowering of the brow. I applied myself to identifying the business end of the shovel and, within minutes, I was excavating a quite well-engineered trench into the snowbank. Hildy watched me anxiously as I worked, and began her little teeter-totter dance as liberty approached. Then as she was led to freedom she mooed a festive song of her own invention.

I sank my shovel into the bank and leaned on it and wiped from my brow the residue of more physical work than I'd done since my rowing days.

"Well, good job we came along when we did, what?"

Sally turned slowly back to me, like one of those Bavarian clockwork figures, just marginally more terrifying.

"I'll take that." She held out her hand and I passed her the shovel. "And I'll thank you, Mister Boisjoly, to in future refrain from interfering with my cow."

"I'm not sure a charge of interfering with livestock is warranted. I merely shared with Hildy a little Christmas cheer."

"You got her drunk."

"My dear Miss Barnstable..." I began the traditional refrain of a man with nothing to say in his defence, but was spared the need to exhaust all variations of "uhm", "ah", and "eh, what?" by Hildy, who was once again mooing a plaintive call. She had stumbled directly into another snowbank.

"You're a fish out of water in this part of the country, aren't you?" said Ivor as we watched Sally, finally, lead Hildy back to her stable.

"A very apt metaphor, Inspector," I agreed. "Indigenous dairy folk probably learn at their mother's knee that cows can't hold their liquor."

"I would have thought that most people, balancing the issues, would err on the side of not feeding mulled wine to a cow."

"Most people wouldn't impersonate the Aga Khan to smuggle a donkey into the winner's circle at Epsom either, but have *you* ever been stuck with a hatpin by the queen mum? The world needs its unconventional thinkers."

"Sometimes, Mister Boisjoly, things are exactly as they appear." Ivor knocked out his pipe meaningfully on his heel. "The only person in Graze Hill who had cause to kill Major Fleming is your aunt, and the tracks in the snow mean that she's also the only person who could have done it."

"I know how it looks, Inspector, but we've found ourselves in this position before."

"Once, yes," admitted Ivor. "When you had the advantage of local knowledge and peculiar circumstances. But this... this is an old-fashioned motive and it's old-fashioned police work that's solved it. It's a crime of passion, that's for certain, and I don't doubt the judge will show leniency. That doesn't mean I'm looking forward to putting your aunt behind bars, but I am looking forward to putting you in your place."

CHAPTER NINE
Zero Zone at the Zeppelin's Zenith

The Feast of Stephen rang out across Graze Hill in the form of church bells, a bright, blue and white morning, and piping hot tea.

"This is uncharacteristically correct, Vickers," I said, casting a suspicious eye over a tray of cream, sugar, cup and saucer, teapot, and a crisp cloth under which I discovered a toasted crumpet dripping with local produce.

I took my tea by the window of the Heath Room next to the glowing brazier. Calm night had given onto tranquil day and had left behind wavy pastures of downy snow, but something else had been deposited onto the scene, something utterly and completely normal, and yet which had been conspicuously absent the day before. I studied the pastoral winter tableau, drinking my tea and focussing all my faculties, but it wasn't until a chorus of hollow clangs echoed across to me that I was able to put my finger on it.

"I say, Vickers, the cows have returned."

"I'm very gratified to hear it, sir," said Vickers, assembling a combination of winter tweeds on the bed.

"Don't you think that's rather peculiar?"

"If I may speak freely, sir, no, I do not. Is it?"

"I confess I'm not sure myself. There were none at all there yesterday afternoon," I said thoughtfully. "Perhaps they had duties elsewhere. Not really my area of expertise, although I am rapidly developing a certain conversant familiarity — resist, by the way, the temptation to buy a cow a drink. She'll thank you for it, have no apprehension about that, but it will end badly."

"I'll take careful note of it, sir."

I flowed with the tidal scent of sausages, bacon, eggs and coffee to the dining room where I encountered Puckeridge, bending over the sideboard, engaged in dabbing a drop of grease away from a silver platter.

"Morning Puckers. Aunty Azalea not yet disinterred?"

"I suspect that Miss Boisjoly has composed a tray for herself," deduced Puckeridge, a bit sniffily, "and retired to her room."

And indeed the orderly arrangements of a latticework of bacon, a pyramid of sausages, an oval of eggs, and a rack of half-a-dozen slices of toast had been spoiled by the absence of one rasher, one banger, a runny sunny-side, and a single slice of toast.

"Quite understandable. Such is the prerogative of the persecuted innocent. Doubtless Jean Valjean would have taken all his meals alone in his room, had he meals. And a room."

"She made it known that she will be home to visitors at midday."

"Then so will I," I said. "I have much business in bustling downtown Graze Hill this morning." I prepared a plate of protein and took my place alone at the table. "Tell me, Puckeridge, do cows like snow?"

"In what sense, sir?"

"All of them. Aesthetically, gastronomically. Whatever comes to you. I note that dozens of them can be seen from my window this morning, where yesterday there were none."

"Cows are very attuned to their daily routine — they are the timepieces of dairy country. I expect that you arrived yesterday at milking time for that particular herd."

"And that mysterious task accomplished, they raced back out to frolic in the snow?"

"I think not," said Puckeridge, diplomatically expressing 'of course not, you citified noddy'. "They would have presented themselves for milking according to schedule, after which they would know that feed troughs would be available in the fields. This is done to allow time to clean the stables, store the milk, and perform general maintenance tasks."

"I see. So, to get a cow to leave a warm stable outside of regular office hours, you'd have to offer it some sort of incentive. Rum-soaked raisins and orange rinds, to pick an example at random."

"I wouldn't advise it, sir."

"Never a wiser word," I said. "Though we may have our differences with regard to the Equal Franchise Act and the current fashion for the faux bob, on this point we are of one mind."

"I'm not sure that I follow, sir."

"I assumed that you were a reformer," I explained. "I didn't see you at church last night."

"The staff find it more convenient to attend morning services," said Puckeridge.

"I didn't realise there were morning services," I said. "I understood there was little point in dairy country."

"It's true that Sunday mornings at Saint Stephen's are somewhat undersubscribed at the best of times, and in the winter even more so."

"Otherwise the same docket, is it?" I asked. "High Anglican readings, homily, communion, etc?"

"I believe that Mister Padget employs the morning services to expand his range, somewhat," said Puckeridge. "He's an admirer of John Mason Neale."

"The reverend songwriter? Chap who gave us *Good King Wenceslas*, about the mad king who bids his page follow his footsteps in the snow so they can spring a load of charity on an unsuspecting serf."

"Yes, sir. Mister Padget has similar ambition and an abiding interest in the story of Saint Stephen. He likes to trial his own poetry with the less discriminating morning congregations."

"You have my sympathies."

"Thank you, sir."

It was one of those clear, crisp Boxing Days that smell the way they look — woodfire smoke drifted lightly on still winds, coming from everywhere and nowhere. The clang of cowbells carried in much the same way, and apart from rare clumps of snow weakening their grip under a morning sun and dropping with a plop from the branches, the landscape might have been a still photograph.

I slipped along the main street, passing the Sulky Cow, which had yet to open, Hildy's manger, at which I glanced longingly, and the church. Little cottages — the *pieds à terre* of the farming community — lay empty and cold and, consequently, almost completely buried in snow. So it was a simple matter to identify the vicarage house, which was near the edge of the village perpendicular to the road, directly facing the townside profile of the church. A path had been worn in the snow from the front door, across the churchyard to the apse entrance.

The house was a pleasant jumble of additions and renovations to what had probably been a modest stone house in the style of the church it served, and had since acquired a porch, which had then been covered and enclosed and given stained-glass doors, and some lumpy growths out the sides and back, styled in the Georgian and Victorian tastes of the eras in which they were built.

Mister Padget himself answered the door, and explained that it would otherwise not have been answered.

"The housekeeper leaves us at Christmas. She has grown children in Ipswich."

"An excellent place for grown children, in my experience. Plenty of high ceilings and open spaces. I've come calling upon Flight-Lieutenant Hern-Fowler — he left me with many questions last night."

"Oh dear," said Padget, taking my coat. "I'm afraid that Monty has gone for a morning constitutional in the woods. I don't know when to expect him back."

"Then I wish to claim my consolation prize — is Mister Millicent on the premises?"

"Ah, yes, he's in the parlour," said Padget with visible relief. "Can I bring you tea?"

"Lashings, if you can spare it." I gestured down the hall toward a source of natural light. "Just down here, is it, the parlour?"

"Yes. Oh, Mister Boisjoly..." Padget said with stagey second-thoughtedness. "Have you had a moment to read over my little effort?"

"Your little what now?"

"The modest oeuvre that I entrusted to you last night," he said sheepishly. "Forgive me. I should have known you would be too busy."

"What I mean to say, Mister Padget, is that you've no business calling it a modest oeuvre or little effort," I said, backfilling quickly. "It's a most erudite composition. It flows and flies and, dare I say it, it inspires. It's a most worthy accomplishment."

"I say, Mister Boisjoly, I'm extremely gratified to hear you say it." Padget flushed and fiddled as though I'd just asked him to be my bride, and he took up his invisible knitting with vigour. "You don't think it a trifle... pretentious?"

"Pretentious?" I affected to weigh the word. "I don't think so, no. I see where you're coming from, there are many bold flourishes, but that's what they are, bold. No, no, I would have to reject all suggestions that the work is pretentious. Now, if you'd suggested that it was sententious, I might entertain the idea, but no, not pretentious."

"I feared that I had taken some liberties with the

rhyming scheme."

"In all frankness, Mister Padget, you did. I noticed it. But you didn't defy the scheme so much as extend it. What masterpiece isn't the result of some rule being broken?"

"Saint Paul's Cathedral?"

"My point exactly," I said. "Did you know that Sir Christopher Wren pioneered a completely new form of geometry to justify the physics of the dome of Saint Paul's?"

"Did he?"

"Might have. The parlour is just down this way, you say."

"Hm? Oh, yes. I'll bring the tea."

The parlour was a long, narrow extension from the back of the house, thick of brick on the outside and made cosy on the inside by deep stained oak, cushioned benches and a crackling fire. An entire wall was composed of three windows and one Cosmo Millicent, pared back to a simple green and red checked dressing gown and purple ascot. His monocle hung from a delicate chain pinned to the pocket of his robe. He sat chewing on a pencil and squinting out onto snowy Main Street, Graze Hill. On the deep sill before him was a stack of papers with nothing on them, and a thesaurus.

I tapped lightly on the door frame as a precaution against giving the absorbed artist a start and costing the literary world some irretrievable jewel.

"Morning, Cosmo."

"Oh, what ho, Anty," he said, dropping his pencil like a bomb onto the papers. "I say, this writing lark's not so easy as it looks from a distance."

"Why don't you tell me what you've got so far?"

Cosmo and I looked at the blank pages.

"What you want is an outline," I said. "Where are these copious notes you took? That's where you should be starting, if I recall my days of writing school papers."

"To be entirely candid, Anty, when I say I 'took' notes, I meant more in the notional sense."

"You mean you didn't write anything down."

"In a nutshell."

I sat on the bench by the fire.

"Perhaps you should," I suggested, "while it's still relatively fresh."

"That's what I've been doing. It's just not coming. I have what I believe is called 'writer's blot'."

"Block," I corrected. "Your problem is you're trying to write your book and recall what your uncle told you at the same time. I submit to you that these are two entirely distinct skills. Just get it down in point form, and decorate it later."

"You think so?"

"I'm sure of it," I said. "In any case it's bound to be more constructive than sitting by the window, gazing at the snow. Tell me the last thing he told you."

"It was just yesterday morning, in fact, at the Sulky Cow," said Cosmo. "He was recounting the night he went down. It was December, as it happens, 1917. Uncle Flaps was a captain, at the time, and commander of a fighter squadron operating out of Dunkirk. It was late at night and they received word that London had been attacked by Zeppelin."

"Monstrous machines."

"Rather. All manner of hell had been unleashed on the capital, it seems, and some half-dozen of the things had simply floated off, scot-free."

"Doubtless laughing maniacally all the way."

"Just so," agreed Cosmo. "So, up they went, into a foggy night over the channel."

"Brave boys."

"Quite. They're up there for hours, though, and just when they think they missed the blighters, the clouds part and there are two of the monstrosities, floating in the air like dark leviathans of the storms."

"Oh, I say, you should write that down," I suggested.

"You think so? It's not mine, if I'm honest, it's one of the major's."

"It's his story."

"Quite so." Cosmo scribbled down the phrase. "Anyhow, in they go, guns blazing. But, turns out, those dashed balloons were fixed with machine guns."

"I think that's widely known."

"Is it?" said Cosmo. "I didn't know it. Nevertheless, my uncle did, and it turned into quite a dance of destiny."

"Another one of the major's?"

"Yes. Worth keeping?"

"Absolutely."

Cosmo added it to his list.

"This goes on for some time, you see, and then one or, probably several of them, hit a sore spot and, ka-boom, like some celestial Christmas cracker."

"Ah, excellent. Doubtless a shell caused a spark."

"Exactly. They were full of helium, you know, Zeppelins."

"Hydrogen, I think you'll find," I gently corrected.

"What do you think of that last one, 'celestial Christmas cracker'?"

"Luke-warm, I think. One of the major's?"

"No, actually, my own."

"Perhaps keep it in reserve," I suggested, "on the rare chance nothing better comes up. Then what happened?"

"Well, that still left one of the devils up there, making a run for home. Our boys give chase, but they're running out of fuel and ammunition at this point. And then a most extraordinary thing happened — one of the chaps, bloke they called Cardiac on account of his breathtaking daring — he actually does run out of ammunition. And, near as my uncle can tell, he seems to think that everyone has, and he decides that he's not letting that Zeppelin live to fight another day — he positions himself above the thing..."

"Dear Lord. He dive-bombed it."

"He did," said Cosmo, now as absorbed by the story as, I realised then, I was. "The major saw what Cardiac was planning and so did the others — there were five planes in total — but they weren't all out of ammunition. So everyone scrambled to put the silver bullet into the heart of the beast before Cardiac could sacrifice his own life. But then..."

"Shall I be mother?" Padget called out as he wheeled in the tea trolley.

"As it comes from the pot, please Vicar."

"The usual, thanks."

Padget distributed cups and saucers and drew our attention to a plate of pre-war, armoured biscuits.

"What are we discussing?" asked the Vicar, taking a pew by the window.

"Cosmo is endeavouring to remind himself of some of the stories the major had shared with him. Today's feature is the Adventure of the Zeppelins."

"Ah, yes," the vicar nodded. "The day he was shot down."

"Blown out of the sky, it turns out," said Cosmo. "So, there they are, everyone racing toward the Zeppelin simultaneously, giving it everything they've got from machine guns to sidearm fire, and somebody apparently hits the sweet spot. Up it goes, just like that. One second the major's flying in almost total darkness, the next he's surrounded by flame, like he's flying through Hell itself."

Cosmo and I shared an unspoken consensus and he took a moment to write down 'flying through Hell itself' before continuing...

"It's too late to pull up or bank out or whatever, so they fly straight into the wreckage. The major, amazingly, comes out the other side, but he's on fire. I don't mean his plane is burning, I mean everything, including the major, is in flames."

"It's a miracle anyone survived," claimed Padget.

"Very few did," said Cosmo. "But the major was in a dive and so he had momentum and a single thought — water. If he could ditch his plane in the sea in the next few seconds he could live to tell the tale."

"What extraordinary presence of mind," I opined.

"He said that being on fire heightens the powers of concentration considerably."

"I rather imagine that it would."

"Anyway, it worked. He hit the water at something like survival speed and his plane broke up, mostly, but he was able to cling to a bit of wing for he couldn't say how long. Some time later, the sun is rising and he's being pulled onto a boat that smells of fish and then and only then does he allow himself to pass out. Next thing he knows he's in an evacuation hospital somewhere in Yser, wrapped from head-to-foot in bandages and being generously medicated with good French brandy. Took him a week to realise he'd lost an eye, and another week to care."

"I say," I commented. "You add a bit of background colour and you've got an entire chapter there."

"Yes, riveting stuff," added Padget.

"Let's have another," I proposed.

"Ah, well, I could do, I suppose," said Cosmo, noncommittally. "There's that time they were escorting a bombing mission. The major got separated from his squadron and when the clouds parted he found himself flying in perfect formation with six German fighters."

"Solid stuff. What happened?"

"Uhm..." Cosmo glanced imploringly at his stack of blank sheets of paper. "Shot his way out of a sticky situation, I think. Dodged, dived, weaved, thrusted. Maybe parried a bit."

"Perhaps what you need, Cosmo, is a ghostwriter. Someone to help you draw all the threads together."

Cosmo put his hands together and shook his head. He closed his eyes to lock down the effect.

"I couldn't possibly do that. I was born to this, Anty. Ever since I learned that I was related to the great Flaps Fleming I knew that it was my life's calling to tell his story."

"Ever since?" I repeated. "How long, roughly, is ever?"

"About six weeks, as it happens. My mother is in America for an extended stay, and I was going through her correspondence, looking for a lighter or something I think, and I came across some old letters. One clue led to another, and I discovered that Mama and the major were cousins."

"She never saw fit to mention it?"

Cosmo shared a meaningful glance with the vicar, who smiled reassuringly.

"Relations with the family have always been a bit wobbly for me," he said. "I expect Mama thought I'd bother him about, well, writing his life story or some such thing."

"Raven-haired ram of the family, are you?"

"I suppose there's a bit of that, yes." Cosmo fiddled distractedly with his pencil and turned his gaze back to the scene beyond the windows. "I've had a couple of false starts. Nothing to be ashamed of, but it's so much easier to acquire a reputation for failing than it is for trying, what?"

"You've had other life's callings?" I asked.

"Nothing like this, of course. I held the British patent for the Trident Precision Timepiece. Have you heard of it?"

"I think not."

"It's a waterproof wristwatch. Accurate to a depth of three hundred feet. Unfortunately, it was only accurate at that depth. On dry land it tended to display random times and was known to run backward."

"Rotten luck."

"Just so," agreed Cosmo. "Pure chance. That was not, however, the view taken by Mama. She swore — in front of a notary, mind — that it would be the last time she financed one of my ventures."

"There were others?"

"One or two. Three if one counts sponsoring a bicycle team in the London to Exeter Rally."

"Isn't London-Exeter a motorcycle race?"

"Which is why I don't count that one."

"Quite rightly, too, in my view."

"Mistake easily made."

"Like falling off a log," I agreed. "But now you've found your vocation. Did you say that your uncle was fully throttle-down about the project?"

"Oh, rather. He was all chips in for the book. And I hadn't even mentioned the Hollywood offer."

"There's been an offer from Hollywood?" I asked.

"Well, no, not in concrete terms, but it only stands to reason, what? Once the book is a roaring success."

"I can't help but think, Cosmo, that you'll want to have settled the legal details before entertaining Hollywood offers." I paused while we all accepted another cup of tea. "Do you know if your uncle left a will?"

Cosmo looked up from the task of blowing steam off his tea. "I'm quite sure he didn't. He was still a young man, by most standards."

"Nevertheless," I said. "Bachelors of a certain age are known to become sentimental about their legacy. I knew of a chap who added a codicil to his will requiring all his descendants be named Evelyn."

"No!"

"Yes!"

"I say," said Cosmo meditatively. "I know the major had a solicitor in Steeple Herding. Chap named Boodle."

"Couldn't hurt to pay him a visit. Make sure that your verbal agreement with Flaps is worth at least the paper it's written on."

"Oh, rather. Sound advice, thanks Anty."

"Don't mention it," I said. "That's *my* vocation. And I have another pearl to bestow. You know, Monty was in your uncle's squadron. Why don't you ask him to fill in the few holes in your copious notes?"

Cosmo raised an eyebrow to the vicar who replied with silent censure. I've seen, in my days, many dark secrets pass wordlessly, and this looked a ripe one.

"What is it?" I asked. "Is he writing a book of his own?"

"No, nothing like that. It's just..." began Cosmo in that way people begin when they hope to be interrupted.

"It's not for us to repeat scurrilous rumour," spake Padget, expressing the wisdom of *his* vocation.

"I fear I must differ with you there, Vicar," I said. "Rumour, particularly of the scurrilous variety, thrives in backhanded whispers. It's from hushed exchanges between feckless chatterboxes that it draws its strength, its venom. Let daylight shine upon these charges, Vicar, and watch them shrivel and die before you. Verily."

Padget eased himself into the role of the easily convinced. "This is entirely groundless, you understand. He finished the war with multiple honours. Stayed on, in fact, while the Royal Flying Corps became the Royal Air Force, and was elevated to Flight-Lieutenant."

"Most admirable. What's the dirt?"

Padget looked furtively about the parlour for spies. "According to the major, there was some question, during the war, of Monty's loyalties."

"You don't mean..."

"Yes, Mister Boisjoly," said Padget earnestly. "A spy."

CHAPTER TEN

The Curious Comportment of the Common Cuckoo

Directly out the front door of the vicarage was the profile of the church and the southern face of the clock, indicating a yawning gap of an hour until lunch time. Also before me was the road home, to my left, and to my right the footprints in the snow of the newly dodgy Flight-Lieutenant Hern-Fowler, winding into the woods, accompanied by the circular impression of a walking stick. My heretofore dormant spy-catcher instincts awoke with a start and off I went in hot pursuit.

I had been tracking my prey across the frozen tundra for about five minutes when I was distracted by a snow owl and my hunt became a pleasant walk in a silent winter wood. The thing about your pleasant walks in silent winter woods is the unblemished symmetry of it all — one old-growth spruce with a coat of winter white looks very much like the next. Consequently, once I was out of view of the village I wasn't so much following Monty's tracks in the snow as relying on them to keep from getting hopelessly lost. In time, I reached the treeline and a familiar view of cows in a snowy meadow, and from there the suspected mole tracks led directly to Herding House.

"Is Flight-Lieutenant Hern-Fowler on the premises, Puckeridge?" I asked as I blew in with a stiff wind.

"He is," said Puckeridge, very nearly cracking a smile. It was gratifying to see the effect the sudden uptick in callers was having on the career butler. "He is in the library with Miss Boisjoly."

"To which Miss Boisjoly do you refer, Puckeridge? I ask, because you certainly can't mean my Aunt Azalea, who would rather stick hot needles in her eyes than entertain strangers in her own home."

"Your aunt relaxed her normally vigorous policy when the flight-lieutenant made it known that he was an old and dear friend of Major Fleming." Puckeridge spoke in proud, confiding tones, as though relating to me some milestone in the development of a toddler of our mutual acquaintance.

"Extraordinary. Is the flight-lieutenant staying for lunch?"

"I believe so." Puckeridge cast an eye almost imperceptibly over my damp tweeds. "But you have plenty of time to change, sir."

"Quite right," I agreed. "Send me the very first Vickers you encounter, will you?"

Minutes later Vickers was fitting me out with a warm and dry herringbone suit over a tan waistcoat.

"Did you happen to see Monty Hern-Fowler sneak aboard, Vickers?"

"No, sir. Mister Padget informed me of his arrival."

"Well, be on your guard if you're introduced," I warned. "Be particularly vigilant about receiving coded messages or being pressed into transporting microfilm."

"I shall keep a keen eye open, sir."

"See that you do. According to the Reverend Padget and the Writer Cosmo, Flaps Fleming claimed that there were whispers that Monty's sympathies were, let us say, divided."

"I find that difficult to believe, sir," said Vickers, flatly. "My understanding is that Major Fleming and Flight-Lieutenant Hern-Fowler were brothers in arms."

"The perfect cover. Anyway, that's what they said. They went on to claim that suspicions were generously distributed by a captured German pilot, who apparently gave credible evidence that the Bosch were in regular receipt of friendly updates of the activities of the squadrons headquartered at Dunkirk."

"Did the prisoner identify the flight-lieutenant by name?"

"Apparently nobody, even unto the court of Kaiser Wilhelm, knew the true identity of the agent known only as 'Cuckoo'."

"A very clever code name."

"It is, yes. I thought so myself," I agreed. "Just to be sure we're on the same page, though, Vickers, why do you find it clever?"

"The Cuckoo lays its eggs in the nests of other birds, who then unknowingly nurse their young."

"Just as the Dunkirk squadron was harbouring a Hun in its bosom."

"Yes, sir."

"Rather convincing story, then."

"Yes, sir," conceded Vickers. "Far from conclusive, though."

"No, I agree, but the chattering classes go on to point out that roughly half of Monty's immediate ancestors hailed from the wrong side of history, and as a boy he spent many a happy summer fishing idly in the Danube and hiking in the Black Forest and, quite possibly for all anyone knows, learning spycraft at the *Allgemeine Kriegsschule*."

"It's hardly unusual to have a German branch in even the best of families."

"Almost a requirement, but now we get to the intriguing part; when the Major related all this he cast Monty in the role of the dearly departed — so far as Flaps Fleming was concerned, his entire squadron, with the notable and obvious exception of himself, died during a heated exchange of views with a Zeppelin. And once Monty was dead — or at any rate presumed to be — the fortunes of the Dunkirk squadron leapt from success to success."

Vickers took the position that any number of explanations could account for this turn of events, and I saw that the defence and prosecution were at loggerheads. I changed lanes.

"Incidentally, Vickers, there was a sheet of paper in the jacket of my swallow-tails. Did you happen to rescue it?"

"Yes, sir," said Vickers with a glance at the little writing desk next to the fire. "I left it out to dry."

"It was in my pocket when I was digging a cow out of a snowbank," I explained. "Is it still legible?"

"I couldn't say, sir."

"Come come, Vickers, you must have glanced at it. It's not like it was in a sealed envelope."

"I may have inadvertently read a few passages," admitted Vickers stoutly.

"Still comprehensible, then?"

"Regrettably, sir, it is."

"That bad, is it?"

"I fear so. May I enquire who authored the piece?"

"Mister Padget," I said. "You wouldn't call it erudite?"

"I would not, no."

"Nor would you contend that it flows, flies, nor inspires?"

"It is a very ambitious lyric, sir. It recounts the events leading to the death by stoning of Saint Stephen."

"Cheerful."

"It appears to be a Christmas carol, and is intended to be sung to the tune of *In dulci jubilo*."

"You're joking."

"Would that I were, sir."

"This is very disturbing, Vickers."

"I'll put it on the fire."

"No, don't do that," I sighed. "Best hand it over. I'm afraid that I gave Mister Padget to believe that I'd read it, and furthermore thought it something just short of Byron's *She Walks in Beauty* but a shade better than Tennyson's *The Lady of Shalott*."

"I understand, sir," said Vickers, though he plainly didn't, because he followed up with, "Might I ask why?"

"Till you're blue in the face, if it gives you any pleasure, but as I don't know myself I won't be able to provide you a satisfactory answer. Youthful indiscretion, perhaps? The man just sprung it on me. He's quite canny for a country vicar."

In that moment the dinner bell gonged an appetising, lunch-time tone, and I followed it to the dining room.

Puckeridge was standing at the dining room door like a sentry. He gave me an approving nod, then swept through the door before me and announced "Mister Anthony Boisjoly" as though he expected it to be followed by trumpets.

I took a quick census of the multitude and worked out that, counting Aunty Boisjoly and Monty Hern-Fowler, there were three of us. Monty was holding a chair for my aunt.

"Ah, there you are, Boisjoly," he whooped, marching over to shake my hand and then take his place at the opposite end of the table.

"Hello Monty, Aunty."

"Monty was a close friend of Flaps," said Aunty Azalea. "He's been entertaining me with some of the most remarkable tales of daring."

"I don't doubt it. Indeed, our mornings were similarly employed." I addressed Monty. "Cosmo Millicent was recounting to me the fateful encounter with the zeppelins over Dunkirk."

"Tragic waste of life." Monty lowered his eyes and shook his head. "Ah! Devilled eggs."

Puckeridge and Alice had returned and the cheerful kitchen maid was presenting a tray of appetisers.

"The way Cosmo tells it," I said, "you didn't survive the ordeal."

"Well how would he know that? He wasn't there. Couldn't have been more than a boy at the time."

"I mean, according to Major Fleming."

"Curious. I have a very clear recollection of the event, and I distinctly remember seeing it through. Landed at *Petite Synthe* with my tail feathers on fire."

"You're not a ghost then."

"Ahhh!" barked Monty with satisfaction. He had been hand-delivering a devilled egg to his mouth but abandoned the consignment and leaned forward. "If it's a ghost story you're after, let me tell you the most extraordinary tale to come from a period in history that spat out legends like they were watermelon seeds."

"Oh, yes, please," gushed Aunty. She also clapped her hands and, I believe, giggled.

"Christmas Day, it was..." Monty moderated his tone to a low, portentous roar. "...just a few weeks after the tangle with the Zeppelins. It was a cold, foggy morning over the channel. Silent. Still."

The dining room, too, was silent and still, and even Puckeridge and Alice stood transfixed by the door.

"Flaps was recovered well enough to be evacuated, and it was decided to profit from the Christmas intermission to bring him home. We took a *Parasol* — little French, mono-wing surveillance plane. Two-seater. No weapon. Useless in combat but we weren't looking for a fight. Just wanted to get the poor blighter home — all covered in bandages, missing an eye, out of his head on whatever they were giving him to kill the pain."

"And you were flying on Christmas Day, under the cover of fog," I added.

"Like pea soup," confirmed Monty. "Something odd about that mist, though. Something unreal about it. It rose from the sea like a solid wall that dared not make landfall. Just hung there, like a beacon of fog, warning, 'don't fly, it's too foggy'."

"But fly you did."

"Best time for it, under normal circumstances." Monty pushed aside his plate and took up his fish knife as a joystick. "I flew directly into it and lost visibility instantly but then, not a mile out to sea, we came out the other side into the clearest, crispest, calmest day for flying you couldn't have hoped for if you'd designed it yourself. Low winds, sun at my back."

"Ah, so the fog misled you," I guessed.

"On the contrary, the threat was far graver than I could have imagined. Halfway across the channel, with Dover in sight, I saw them." Monty eased up on the fish knife and squinted into the distance at a disquieting menace posed by the floral table centrepiece.

"Oh, dear," shuddered Aunty Azalea. "Was it Jerry?"

"It was. Two red devils from the infamous Jasta Eleven. The most cold-blooded, precision predators in the air at the time. The rear guard of a bombing mission, as it turned out. Otherwise they'd no doubt have observed convention."

"Which convention is that, Monty?" I asked.

"We were an unarmed observation craft, heading home. It was Christmas Day. As they approached, I gave them a smart salute, expecting it to be returned and for that to be the end of it. Instead they just buzzed by, dangerously close, on either wing, without so much as a nod."

"How unforgivably Teutonic."

"I learned later that the bombing mission was a bust — they were chased away from London and forced to jettison their payload in the sea. By an extraordinary turn of luck they scored a direct hit on one of their own U-boats."

"And presumably they hoped to keep it between themselves," I guessed.

"Precisely. Sure enough, I heard their engines accelerate and when I looked back they'd both climbed to twelve thousand feet and were banking back..." Monty looked over his shoulder to confirm the position of enemy fighters, "...positioning themselves to come at us out of the sun."

"Rather unsporting strategy to take with a sitting duck, isn't it?" I asked.

"I doubt they knew any other way, the blighters."

"What did you do?" squealed Aunty Azalea, now quite literally on the edge of her seat and kneading her napkin with both hands.

"The only thing I could do." Monty scanned the table for suitable cloud cover. "I ran for it. I spotted a raggedy bit of cumulus hovering at about five thousand feet, and I dived into it." He struggled with the fish knife as the dining room table met unexpected crosswinds. "Immediately banked sharpish, hoping to double back on the sons of bachelors. But when I came out of the cloud, there they were, right in front of us and bearing down fast. I fancied I could see them taking aim."

"Oh my goodness," said Aunty, as though there was a chance that Monty's story ended badly.

With calm deliberation, Monty levelled us off at about forty-five hundred feet. "I said to Flaps, well old man, we had a good run. I suppose we'll be joining Cardiac, Mush, and Tippy sooner than expected. Won't they be surprised to see us! On Christmas Day, no less."

"Your late colleagues?" I surmised.

"Second Lieutenant Carwyn Rhys-Thomas, Second Lieutenant Morris MacIntosh, Lieutenant Terrence Mountjoy. Best lads to ever recover a spin and come up shooting." Monty chose that moment to glance out the window and use his napkin to address some issue he had with his eyes. "They all three died the day we took on those Zeppelins." Monty's normally booming voice reduced momentarily to an emotional croak. "Sacrificed themselves for each other. And for Flaps and me."

"We're very glad they're still waiting to see you, at least, Monty," I said.

Monty turned back to the table and leaned onto it.

"That's just it, my boy," he said.

"What is?"

"There we were, screaming toward destiny at full throttle. The Bosch had us dead to rights. Then, on a tuppence, they both pitched into a deliberate spin, dropped about a thousand feet and decamped like they were fired out of a cannon."

"How peculiar."

"Never a truer word, Boisjoly. As peculiar as anything you've ever seen," said Monty with solemn satisfaction. "We went into that cloud alone, but we came out in battle formation with the very best wingmen that heaven could spare. Cardiac, Mush, and Tippy had come back to escort us home one last time."

Aunty Azalea burst into tears. Alice laughed that delighted laugh that one employs when seeing a bully slip on some ice. Even Puckeridge put his shoulders slightly further back, as though working through a cold shiver.

"We exchanged a long, last salute," continued Monty. "And then they peeled away. And then... then they were gone." Monty looked down at his fish knife and once more mourned three brave boys.

Silence reigned, apart from Aunty happily weeping. I reflected on whether or not now was the right moment to ask Monty if he was a German spy and decided, on balance, that it was not.

In the next instant Monty snapped back to the present, popped an entire devilled egg into his mouth, and said, "Of course, their deaths only fed the rumours that there was a spy amongst us."

"A spy, Monty?" I said, aghast. "Not really."

"Of course not really," he said. "It was a counter-intelligence operation by the Germans. We had the same sort of brief — if you're ever captured and you feel you must tell the enemy something, tell them that the Americans have managed to recruit an agent on the kaiser's kitchen staff, or that the navy has developed an airborne contaminant that cuts cabbage yields in half. Anything to sow confusion and cause the Bosch to waste their time."

"And this particular ruse targeted you."

"Me? No, of course not. Where did you get that idea?"

"I mean, you, as in the squadron. The collective you."

"Ah, quite. I take your meaning," Monty acceded. "Dunkirk had its share of rotten luck, just like everywhere else at the time. So the filthy slander that one of us was tipping off the Hun got more credibility than it deserved, which of course was none at all."

"Of course."

"There weren't five more British lads in the entire armed forces. Flaps was from Hertfordshire. Dairy country, for pity's sake. Went directly from making kites out of parcel paper and pine twigs to Balloon Section."

"Were you all flyboys by calling?" I asked, slyly manoeuvring the conversation around to pre-war skiing conditions in the Hornerdörfer.

"Don't be absurd," scolded Monty. "Until the war the state of the art in powered flight was still the Wright Brothers' bicycle shop. Mush MacIntosh was a mechanic in Glasgow. Farm machines. Hadn't even seen an aeroplane until he signed up to keep them flying. Left a wife and two daughters behind, poor chap."

"And Cardiac?"

"Three wives."

"He was certainly doing his part, but I meant with respect to his background."

"That's the majesty of service, Boisjoly." Monty leaned away from the table to allow Alice to clear and replace his cockpit. He leaned toward me again over a *demi filet de sole meunière* and *ris au safran*. "Their backgrounds didn't matter. Tippy Mountjoy was a clubman — theatre, dinner parties, Monte Carlo, anything but work. A waster. Sort of bludger who needed someone to steam-iron his handkerchiefs..."

As he said this, Monty's eyes settled conspicuously on my own crisply pressed and plaited pocket triangle. "...Never did a thing for anyone but himself until he put on a uniform. Cardiac was the same — a womaniser and a gambler, joined up to escape his mounting debts. But wing-to-wing with brothers in arms, they were the bravest, most selfless, stoutest hearts to ever polish a brass button."

"And Flaps?"

"Eh?"

"Major Fleming."

"Even worse," barked Monty. "Family owns practically everything you can see for miles around, you know. He had a duty to these people, but he always thought he was too good for them. Wouldn't even associate with the locals. Took to flight the way a previous generation would have taken to mountaineering or big game hunting — to set himself apart from the lower classes. In command of a squadron, though, he came into his own."

"But did he ever dig a cow out of a snowbank?"

"Not to my certain knowledge, no," answered Monty distantly.

"Well, heroism takes many forms, as you no doubt know. And what of Montgomery Hern-Fowler? What is his story of noble reformation?"

"Ah, well, in dear old Monty, you have the worst scoundrel of them all."

CHAPTER ELEVEN
Sainted Stephen's Sticky End

Despite my subtle gamesmanship, I was unable to draw from Monty a confession that he was a traitor to his class and country. He was much more responsive to my aunt's expression of the famous Boisjoly charm in the form of swooning sighs and the random but judiciously deployed 'tell me more's. Of course, this only generated more tales of daring, including a variation on Flaps' adventure in which he found himself flying in formation with an enemy squadron. I assume it's the sort of thing that happened pretty much on rotation during the Great War.

And so it was that I was feeling decidedly fifth-wheelish. I had never seen Aunty Azalea so immersed in anything that wasn't a velvet curtain, and I don't mind saying that I was rather moved by the scene.

Angling for an excuse, I remembered, with a twinge above the left temple, Padget's opus. I claimed that I had to have a look at it before seeing the Vic later that evening. Aunty and Monty gave me leave with little dissent, though, and I doubtless could have told them that I was late for an appointment to have my head shaved and elaborately tattooed for exactly the same effect.

I returned to my room initially with the intention of laying on a few more layers before facing the cold, but when I spotted the vicar's Christmas carol on the nightstand I felt a pang of whatsit — no doubt the Germans have a word for it — that dread one feels for a moral duty in equal measure of the guilt one experiences for feeling that way.

It was every bit as diabolical as Vickers had described it. I believe that "ambitious" was the sweet-tea euphemism he employed and it was certainly that, with knobs on, but it also appeared to presume a lavish intimacy with the Book of Acts on the part of the listener. The story, in broad strokes, is that Stephen was gadding about Jerusalem like he'd bought the place, putting the wind up any community elder who'd give him the time of day. Casting about for a wheeze to chivvy Steve's wicket, the local nibs settled on fitting him up for a charge of blasphemy.

Standing accused before the Sanhedrin, a sort of borough council of the day, he didn't deny all charges or claim to have been acting under the unfamiliar influence of strong drink, as I might have done, but instead took the opportunity to inventory God's blessings on the nation. Let us assume that was, as a defence argument, neutral. But Stephen's closing act was a vision of God in his heaven with the messiah — a controversial character in the Holy Land at the time — at his right hand. This would have been, technically, blasphemous, and hence a dubious defence against a charge of blasphemy.

So Stephen was carried off by a mob, who doubtless later regretted the rashness of their behaviour, to a place of execution outside the city. They took off their coats, presumably to free up their pitching arms, and laid them at the feet of a bystander who later turned out to be Saint Paul. This is relevant for some reason which for the moment escapes me. Stephen used his last moments to ask God to have mercy on his persecutors, which was quite sporting, because in the next moment they had at him with all manner of jagged rock. The story of Good King Wenceslas it most decidedly is not.

Padget's contribution to the insatiable market for new Christmas melodies was this grisly tale expressed as rhyming couplets and put to the tune of a mediaeval German spiritual. On its own that's hardly a fatal blow to the career prospects of a Christmas carol — we know that *Hark, the Herald, Angels Sing* started life as an ode to the development of the printing press, of all things, and the school convocation favourite *Oh, Christmas Tree* was initially a biting diatribe against a fickle-hearted female. Padget's lyric raised the bar considerably, though, and was ostentatiously sticky in almost exactly the same way *God Rest Ye Merry Gentlemen* isn't.

I was musing on how best to rephrase 'tasteless and baffling' as constructive criticism when there was a discreet tap at the door followed by an equally discreet Vickers.

"Ah, Vickers, excellent timing," I said. "I'm rather at loose ends with regards this giddy song of woe by O. Padget, Bach. of Div."

"I was remiss, sir. I meant to propose putting it on the fire."

"You did. And I like it. It's bold and direct. The only flaw in this otherwise waterproof plan is that it leaves me underprepared should the vicar wish to continue our discussions of the piece tonight, a likely contingency, in light of the generous praise I so rashly lavished on this atrocity. Listen to this first verse...

> *Famed far and wide for charity*
>
> *Not to mention perspicacity*
>
> *Saint Stephen spread the word of God*
>
> *In a manner many found quite odd"*

Vickers visibly winced. "Yes, sir. That verse had, unfortunately, lingered in memory."

"I don't doubt it," I said. "And that's not the worst bit."

"I concur."

"No, I mean, there are portions that were rendered illegible during my heroic battle with the snowbank. What do you make of this..."

> *Saint Stephen was accu-u-used*
>
> *Quite falsely was abu-u-used*
>
> *He was dragged before the Sanhedrin...*

I can't make out the next bit."

"Who accused him of eternal sin?" suggested Vickers.

"Well, it fits," I said, appraising the offence like a demonic crossword puzzle. "Not quite scaly enough, though, by the standards of the rest of this drivel."

"Might I propose, sir, simply standing by your initial appraisal?"

"Persist in pitching porkies, you mean? That sounds cowardly, Vickers, and ideal. Mind you, it's going to be a trial repeating all that adulation with a straight face, now I've read the thing."

"Nevertheless, it strikes me as the strategy least likely to stimulate further discussion of the work."

"Probably true," I said, folding the lyric safely out of view in my pocket. "And what could possibly go wrong?"

The sky, snow and sun had stayed largely with the programme laid out that morning and provided a clear winter backdrop to my walk to the barren no-man's land that is the border between Graze Hill and Steeple Herding. The effect was inclement warmth, and by the time I'd plodded to the frontier I was as breathless and clammy as I'd have been crossing a wheat field in midsummer. At the top of the hill I was rewarded once again with a sweeping view of winter in Hertfordshire including the town of Steeple Herding and its railway station, resembling from that perspective a scale model train set complete with tiny working signals and level crossing, and a miniature dangerous patch of ice in front of the little post office. Closer at hand, set snugly into the woods, was a winsome cottage of rude stone, a thatched roof, and the familiar blue beacon light denoting the building as the constabulary shared by the two villages. I knocked on the door and, in a matter of two ticks, it was swung open by Inspector Wittersham.

"Oh, it's you," said Ivor, with the nasally impatience of a man with a cold answering a door on a winter's day. "Best come in then."

Constable Kimble had managed to make of his home and office a space that was somehow neither. Ivor, wrapped in a becoming shawl of some whiskery weave, bade me sit at a table that also served as a work desk, while he topped up the kettle from a pump at the back wall. That, and an iron coal stove, appeared to amount to kitchen facilities in the little cottage. There was also a broad wooden filing cabinet which doubled as linen storage and, to offset the officious tone with a touch of home, a small but serviceable jail cell.

Ivor clattered another cup and saucer onto a mismatched tumble of a tea set and fell heavily into the chair opposite.

"Where's the constable?" I asked, quite sure that, had he been there, I'd have noticed.

"On his farm," said Ivor. In fact, he quite clearly said "Ob hid farb", but I worked out the subtext in an instant.

"Touch of hay fever, Inspector?"

Ivor looked up at me from the teacup from which he had been inhaling hot vapours.

"I have a cold," he said, as haughtily as he could manage without non-aspirated consonants, which isn't really very haughtily at all.

"You don't fancy building a snow fort then. The sun's been at it all morning and it's peerless packing snow."

"What are you doing here, Mister Boisjoly?"

"Reporting in, Commandant. I bring detailed communiqués from the enemy encampments."

"What enemy encampments?" Ivor was rubbing his forehead, now, as though some new influence was worsening his condition.

"The vicarage, chiefly," I replied. "Did you know that Monty Hern-Fowler was a spy?"

"Is he?"

"Not to be pedantic, but I didn't say that he is a spy, I said that he was a spy."

"Was he?"

"I don't know," I admitted. "According to the vicar and

135

Cosmo Millicent, the major thought he might have been. The story goes that the squadron was experiencing all sorts of uncanny misfortune that could have been attributed to a Cuckoo in the nest."

"A what?"

"A Cuckoo bird. They lay their eggs in the nests of other birds. Rather cold-hearted survival mechanism, as it goes, but I expect they know best."

"Returning to the matter of spies, if you can manage it..."

"Monty practically confessed to me," I said. "I mean, he didn't so much confess as deny that there was a spy at all, but he took the position that he was the worst of a formidably bad lot."

"How many suspects is that now, Mister Boisjoly?" Ivor sneezed and then blew his nose in a kerchief that looked entitled to a military pension. "Mister Trimble killed the major to steal his reputation, I believe... his nephew murdered him for the rights to tell his life story... the blacksmith wanted revenge when the major failed to finance his conkers venture..."

"Yo-yo."

"...his yo-yo factory, as you say... the vicar resented the unfulfilled promise to do up the church... Soaky Mike regarded the victim as a rival for charity drinks... Sally Barnstable, you'll have to help me out with this one, she objected to him drawing trade to her pub?"

"Her father's pub, I think you said."

"Indeed. Makes all the difference. Is there anyone in Graze Hill that you don't suspect, apart from your aunt?"

"Yes," I replied swiftly and certainly. "I believe Hildy the cow to be as pure as the driven snow."

"That leaves only your aunt's staff, who can all account for one another's movements. And your aunt. Face it, Mister Boisjoly, whatever confused theories you're able to invent, at the end of the day, it's your aunt's footprints in the snow."

"And the major's."

"Precisely." Ivor stirred his tea until the spoon was once again available to be stabbed in my direction. "And so the only possible explanation for the circumstances around the murder of Major Aaron Fleming is that your aunt visited him yesterday morning, after he'd been to the pub, where he gave everyone to understand that he was leaving Graze Hill. Doubtless he told Miss Boisjoly the same thing, and that there was no future in their romance, the very romance upon which she had been resting her last hopes of matrimony. She responded as do so many women scorned."

"Then why tell me she'd seen him that morning? And why not make some effort to cover her tracks, literally and figuratively?"

"Are you suggesting that the damning evidence against your aunt is evidence of her innocence?" asked Ivor. "No one is suggesting that she's a criminal mastermind. This was clearly a crime of passion."

This verdict seemed to cheer the inspector, somewhat, and he closed his eyes and sipped his tea in dreamy contemplation of the prospect of hanging my Aunty Azalea.

"Did you say 'farm?'"

"Hmm? No, I didn't say 'farm'."

"You did," I persisted. "When I asked you where Kimble was. You said that he was on his farm."

"Yes, that's right. He has a small holding on the Steeple Herding side of the hill. Why?"

"I'm not sure," I confessed. "Just strikes me as peculiar, a constable having a farm. Like a vicar having a motorcycle, or a cat having a dog."

"It's just a patch, apparently. He doesn't work it so much as shore it up against the ravages of nature. He's there today digging out an earth cellar that collapsed under the weight of the snow."

"Why doesn't he just sell it?"

Ivor recovered his usual, distempered demeanour.

"You're going to make something of it that isn't there."

"Not if you don't give me a fighting chance, I won't."

"Very well." Ivor put down his cup and straightened his shawl. "Constable Kimble doesn't technically own the property. The lease — a ninety-nine year lease — was left to him by an uncle, but according to the antediluvian legal mechanism that all these small towns seem to preserve like clutter in the attic, Major Fleming had first right of refusal on the property."

"Which, presumably, he chose to exercise."

"Not at all." Ivor pointed his teaspoon at me in a manner suggestive of a duel. "This is why I say there's nothing to it. Major Fleming had yet to respond to the option, one way or the other. Kimble wants to take on the property, but the major's procrastination suited him nicely. You see, the constable wishes to marry."

"Yes, I could see how a long lead time would be of service to that end," I said. "Delightful chap, first bloke you'd want on hand if you needed to, say, lift a house so you could sweep under it, but I expect that finding the woman to measure up to him would comprise patience and good old fashioned legwork."

"Don't be an ass, Boisjoly," said Ivor in that flat, uninflected sort of way in which one says 'Don't be a teapot' to a teapot. "He wants to marry Sally Barnstable. Stop it."

"Stop what?"

"Stop thinking that Constable Kimble and Sally Barnstable conspired to kill the major and fit your aunt up for the crime."

"I say, that's uncanny," I said. "Now I'm thinking of a colour..."

"Sally Barnstable won't leave her father alone in the pub, so until it's sold or otherwise disposed of she won't marry. Kimble can't raise the capital to do up the farm, which they intend to one day establish as a sort of breeding ground for that absurd little cow."

"I'll ask you to withdraw that slur, Inspector," I said, pouring myself another cup. "More tea?"

Ivor shoved his cup toward me and I topped it up. "What you want, Inspector, is a warm brandy, or a hot cup of that festive petrol from the Sulky Cow."

"I know," agreed Ivor. "Kimble's teetotal. There's not a drop in the house."

"I say, really? Inspector, in all candour, are you quite certain that Kimble's not a crazed murderer?"

"He just doesn't drink. Perfectly normal."

"We disagree on many things," I said, munificently, "let this be one of them. But he also doesn't go to church. A little odd, that, for an abstemious constable."

"Yes he does, just not in Graze Hill. He goes to Saint Bartholomew's in Steeple Herding."

"Why not alternate? He lives literally on the border."

"Apparently the locals are somewhat clannish, to hear Kimble tell it. A state of affairs brought on by the railway."

"The age-old tale of the lover's triangle," I lamented. "Two towns vie for the affections of the railway station but, alas, she can have only one. If I've seen it once I've seen it a thousand times."

"Worse than that, actually. The residents of Graze Hill were against the railway in its entirety. They felt — correctly, as it turned out — that a railway would undermine the value of the canal, which did most of its business through Graze Hill. For centuries anyone wanting to trade with the capital had to first strike a deal with the village."

"They're still not over it?"

"The railway's only been here twenty years," said Ivor. "And apparently it attracted everything worth having to Steeple Herding — bank, post office. All but one pub. Twenty years ago it was Graze Hill that was the bigger town."

"Well, then, they can't either of them have been a megalopolis," I observed. "And to this day never the twain shall meet?"

"Not even to attend high mass."

"Probably because they don't know what they're missing," I mused. "Come for the sacrilegious golden calf, stay for the stoning of Saint Stephen, put to rhyme."

"The what?"

"Like the calf, it's something you have to see for yourself.

By the way, you can't think of a word that rhymes with Sanhedrin, can you?"

"Mandolin?"

"I'll take it under advisement." I finished the last of my tea, rose, and began battening down the outerwear. "I understand that the major wasn't so strict about mixing with the great unwashed beyond the borders of Graze Hill."

Ivor shrugged into his shawl. "Stands to reason. He was the last of the line of local landowners. He had claims to property on both sides of the divide. What's your point?"

"Did you know he had a solicitor in Steeple Herding?"

"Are you saying there's a will?" Ivor squinted narrowly at me, as though trying to bring me into focus.

"Will, codicil, secret endowment of an expedition to the North Pole... I don't know, Inspector, but if you find this solicitor, we can ask him."

CHAPTER TWELVE
The Debutante Aunt's Debut

Somehow the walk back to Herding House was roughly twice as far as the outbound journey, an anomaly I put down to the arctic headwind that had since taken up a defensive line. Similarly, the sky had clouded over into a steely, unfriendly grey that looked cold to the touch. The temperature had dropped accordingly, from a mid-day high of perhaps forty Fahrenheit to just a few degrees below a strong reminder to dress for winter in the countryside. The aforementioned packing snow, which had softened and glistened beneath a beaming noonday sun, was now so traumatised by this snap change in the weather that it had developed a hard, cynical shell of treacherous ice.

Such was the state of the terrain when I arrived at the Graze Hill crossroads from which, uphill, stood Herding House, and downhill lay the village. Despite my best efforts at alpine trekking, I was gravity's plaything, and I slid gracefully backward all the way to the front door of the Sulky Cow.

Sally cast me a wary eye as I entered, but nodded

cordially and said "Evening, Mister Borgia."

"Good evening, Miss Barnstable. Mike, Cosmo." Soaky Mike and Cosmo were sat at opposite sides of the fireplace, gazing into the flames thirstily and thoughtfully, respectively.

"Cup of your finest seasonal anaesthetic," I said, snapping a shilling onto the bar. I took my cup to the cauldron, ladled myself a portion, and claimed a stool across from Cosmo. He had his thumbs hooked into the pockets of a green waistcoat under a discreet yellow drape-cut jacket. On the table between us were an abridged version of his stack of blank papers and his thesaurus.

"How are the recollections coming along?" I asked.

"A bit sluggish, at the moment, actually, Anty, but I've had rather a topping flash." Cosmo leaned over his cup, set his hands either side of it, and regarded me with an 'are you ready for this?' intensity. "I've decided to stay on a bit."

"At the Sulky Cow?"

"Graze Hill," he specified. "Well, mainly the pub, yes. The game plan is roughly this — my uncle shared most of his stories with everyone here at one time or another, what? So, if I linger on, I'll be able to collect them all, put them in order, apply the old thesaurus, and I'm off the races, what?"

"Most ingenious, Cosmo. Now all that remains is the question of copyright."

"I've had a thought about that, too, actually." Cosmo cast a suspicious eye at Soaky, who was watching the cauldron with a lover's longing. "I have what's called a verbal contract, what? All I need to do is make it stick, somehow, and for that what do I need?"

"A witness?"

143

"A witness, exactly. And who better than an alderman and local business owner?"

"Everett Trimble heard your uncle agree to let you write and sell his life story?" I asked.

Cosmo pursed his lips pensively. "I think it's more accurate to say that he was on hand when it was strongly implied. I feel quite confident that he'll back up my claim."

"Well, that's an enormous relief. Why, though, out of curiosity?"

"It's in the best interests of the town, what? I'll put it to him as a sort of joint venture. The book — and, in due season, the Hollywood picture — re-ignites interest in Flaps Fleming, in turn raising the profile of Graze Hill and its resident business owners and aldermen."

"Most ingenious, Cosmo." I raised my cup of concentrated Christmas in a toast. "Why stop at Everett, though? Why not claim that the entire town heard your uncle's unequivocal commitment to developing his life story into a Hollywood epic?"

"Verisimilitude," said Cosmo, tapping his thesaurus. "More believable if it's one, reliable witness, what? Besides, he's an impressive force, is Everett Trimble. He knows everything about this town and he's got a sort of..." Cosmo glanced quizzically at his sources, "...get-things-doneness about him, what?"

"Speaking of valuable resources, did Monty tell you his ghost story?"

Cosmo started at the question, understandably, because in the very instant I posed it a woeful wail came at us from all directions, as though the walls themselves were lamenting the sins they'd heard overheard across the centuries.

"What the devil was that?" said Cosmo.

Soaky Mike laughed slyly and shook his head, like one who knew precisely what the devil that was. Sally clanged out from behind the bar with a metal bucket and stalked across the floor but then stopped at the door to say "I suppose you know this is you're doing" to me. "She's been like this all day."

"Is that Hildy?" I asked.

"As if you didn't know. Poor thing's got a historic hangover, thanks to you."

Soaky Mike chuckled all the more, not so much in sympathy, but rather in bemused reproof of this current generation of milksop livestock.

"Don't let him near that pot," Sally added, pulling open the door.

Cosmo and I glanced at the clock and took careful note of the time — six o'clock almost to the second.

"Until when?" we asked in unison.

"Until never!" said Sally like an oath sworn from the dock of Bow Street Magistrates Court. She went out and the door followed her as far as the frame, against which it clapped like a stiff slap across a damp cheek.

"She don't mean that," said Soaky, without a moment's hesitation.

"We're going to operate under the assumption that she does," I replied.

"Seems the safer course, what?" said Cosmo, then to me he added the colour commentary, "Soaky's on probation, apparently. Did you two go on a bender with Hildy last night?"

"That is a gross exaggeration," I said, coolly. "It was barely a social tipple, between friends, observing the season."

"Sally makes out like you and Mike took her cow on a wild tear through the fleshpots of Soho. What's this about a ghost story?"

"It's a corker, if you haven't heard it. Voyage with me, now, through the corridors of time, to Christmas morning, 1917..."

"Oh, right, when the squadron came back from the dead to frighten off a pair of unsporting Bosch." Cosmo had taken up his pencil and was idly practising dedications on an otherwise blank sheet of paper.

"You speak rather blithely, I must say, about an eyewitness account of a modern miracle."

"You believe it then?"

"Of course not."

"No, nor I," said Cosmo. "Funny thing — I don't think the major believed it either."

"But he was, ostensibly, present for the proceedings."

"Well, exactly." Cosmo traced a version of his signature that was just his initials in broad cursive. "Monty recounted the ordeal yesterday morning, but the major had never mentioned it, so far as I know, and he appeared to be, I don't know... humouring Monty."

"That seems an odd tone for men with a battle-tested bond," I observed. "They didn't fall on each other's necks as brothers reunited?"

"Not as such, no," said Cosmo, adding a bold underline to his initials, extending from the tail of the M. "Initially, in fact, Uncle Flaps seemed genuinely surprised to see Monty in the flesh. At the risk of belabouring the theme, it was a bit like he was seeing a ghost."

"Was your uncle not expecting Monty?"

"I'd have thought so. I knew he was coming, so you'd think the major would have."

"How did you know?"

"Mister Padget mentioned it." Cosmo spelt out, simply, 'COSMO!' and then quickly crossed it out. "Monty wrote to him to reserve a room."

"But you say that your uncle thought that the major was dead," I reminded him.

"In so far as that's how he described the encounter with the Zeppelins, yes."

"You know what that means, then, I take it?"

"That Monty is a ghost?"

"No," I said. "Well, possibly. That remains to be seen, of course. No, I mean you're missing a trick, not including a chapter on spirits."

"You think I ought?"

"People like ghost stories," I said. "And it would go some distance in backing up my aunt's claim to have seen your uncle's body in the early hours yesterday morning."

"You still haven't sorted that out then."

"I've a couple of working theories," I said, "but they all share the same obscure flaw."

"Which is?"

"They're impossible. There's the timing issue, which I suppose I could budget for by assuming that Aunty Azalea was out of her mind on absinthe, but that still leaves the vexing problem of the footprints in the snow."

"And this inspector bloke is content to hang fire?"

"Not really," I said. "I expect if he didn't have a nasty head cold he'd have nicked my aunty already, but I think he's willing to keep the investigation open until I've thoroughly made a fool of myself."

"What a nuisance," said Cosmo. "I was quite hoping for a chance to go through my uncle's things."

"Your concern is moving, Cosmo."

"Oh, right. I'm sure the real killer will be flushed out and all that, of course. It's just, publishing's a finicky field, what? It's a tragedy all round, but it's also a lovely bit of ballyhoo, as we say in the industry. I need to strike while the iron is hot. Get the manuscript into the hands of discriminating publishers while Uncle Flaps' murder is still in the headlines, what?"

"Well, here's a radical suggestion, then, Cosmo — write the thing. What do you want to be going through your uncle's things for?"

"Background colour. Medals, photographs, letters, commissions, that sort of thing." Cosmo started a new signature, this time a stacked version of his name in block letters. "Of course, we'd already been through it all, many times, but as mentioned I was a bit remiss with the note-taking. Didn't know I was under starter's orders, as it were."

"Just a tick, Cosmo. Are you telling me that when you visited with your uncle at Tannery Lodge you were shown his memorabilia?"

"Sure. Of course. Why not?"

"Because, Cosmo, it's gone. Every bit of it."

The night sky was clear. The wind was still. The temperature had shifted slightly from 'cold for a winter's eve' to 'cold for a winter's eve on a dinghy in the North Sea'. The moon shone brightly and the ice-hill that stood between me and Herding House glistened ominously, much as I expect the summit of Everest glistened before George Mallory on his third and final ascent. The hill had gotten higher, since last viewed, and appreciably more slippy, so I approached through the crackling wood, lurching from tree to tree.

"Lead me to the fire, Puckeridge," I said, shimmying in through the door. "Or, be a good chap, just set me alight where I stand."

We compromised on a warm brandy in the library. Puckeridge brought me a generous snifter the size of a deep-sea diver's helmet while I shivered to a stop before the fire.

"Thank you, Puckeridge. Is my aunt joining me for cocktails before dinner?"

"Miss Boisjoly has dined, sir..." Puckeridge's eyebrow twitched and he had to look away momentarily and swallow before continuing. "...with Flight-Lieutenant Hern-Fowler..." had I not known for an absolute certainty that it was impossible, I'd have said I saw a tear in his eye. "...and Mister Padget, sir."

"My aunt had company? For dinner?"

Puckeridge could only nod energetically to this. In his joy at realising his life's purpose he had lost the power of speech.

"Well that's very jolly," I said. "Are they still in the dining room?"

Puckeridge cleared his throat and composed himself.

"Madame has gone to church, sir. She asked me to tell you that she looks forward to you joining her there."

"In all seriousness, Puckeridge, when she left, presumably with this Hern-Fowler cove and the vicar, did either of them have a gun to her head?"

"Miss Boisjoly was in very good spirits, sir, and very much looking forward to this evening's services as, might I add, are the entire staff."

"The whole household is going, is it?"

"We wouldn't miss it, sir."

"Well, then, I suppose I shouldn't either," I resigned. "Tell me, Puckeridge, how did the Arctic survey team get from here to Saint Stephen's? Dogsled?"

"Mister Barking came by with his sleigh."

"Excellent. When is the next scheduled departure? Have I time for a quick *rotis de boeuf avec son jus* or a simple Dover Sole *amandine*? Doesn't matter if there's no more of that *Meursault* on hand, any Burgundy will do."

"I can do a sandwich board, sir, but the kitchen staff has already left for church, and I fear that Mister Barking will not be making another journey tonight — he's verger of Saint Stephen's."

"Oh, very well, bring on the bread and water while I dress for the odyssey," I said. "Incidentally, Puckeridge, speaking as an expert in the two related fields, how long should one expect a bovine hangover to endure?"

"I've never heard of such a thing, sir."

"Yes, I suppose I have rather broken new ground lately," I confessed. "Imagine a cow, the rough size, shape, and constitution of Hildy the Graze Hill Golden. Now imagine this cow were to consume the dregs of a bucket of mulled wine. What would be the prognosis?"

Puckeridge gave his left eyebrow leave to levitate of its own accord.

"A fully-grown Graze Hill Golden weighs on average seven hundred pounds, Mister Boisjoly. It would take appreciably more alcohol than you or I could drink in a week to have even the slightest effect."

"Any given week, Puckeridge, or does this exclude boat race night?"

"It's a rough formula, sir, but broadly applicable."

"So, in your expert view, I'm cleared of all charges. I may need you to testify to that in the court of public opinion."

"If it's with respect to Miss Barnstable and Hildy, sir, I would prefer not."

The Feast of Saint Stephen is obviously a red-letter day at Saint Stephen's church in Graze Hill, and Mister Padget had pushed the boat out. On either side of the entrance was a wicker torch, lighting the freshly swept steps which had been strewn with golden tinsel. The doorway was trimmed with holly or ivy or whichever it is of those two that has berries. Inside the church, each aisle had its own kerosene lantern and every candle was lit, so a warm, orange glimmer billowed through the doorway and onto the snow like fluid mirth. The vicar stood in the glow, draped in mauve and ivory, and smiling brightly. Had they been in season, I've no doubt he would have had daisies in his hair.

As I arrived Barking was clapping his hands in the cold, rushing the entire Christmas population of Graze Hill inside. I stopped to shake Padget's hand and pop off a little seasonal soft soap.

"Mister Boisjoly," he said, gripping my hand like it posed a danger to himself and others. "May I say again how very gratified I am for your assistance with my little carol."

His eyes glistened as he said this, and I saw in them the wisdom of Vickers' proposal that I stand by my original ovation. What possible value could there be in crushing the man's spirit, especially on the feast day of the patron saint of his own church.

"It's a genuine honour to have been asked, Mister Padget," I said. "I only hope that, in my modest way, I contribute something to the general acceptance of your work among the Christmas classics, the progress of which I will follow with consuming interest."

"You're very kind, Mister Boisjoly." Padget finally released my hand so that he might point toward the front of the church. "Your aunt is just there, next to Monty. Isn't this a grand occasion?"

I had to confess that it was certainly notable. Aunty Boisjoly, whose dislike of human interaction was such that she would avoid mirrors except in time of emergency, was perched on a pew at the very front of the church, chatting merrily with Monty and Everett.

I looked away, of course, and took the precaution of rubbing my eyes, but when I again took in the scene it was every bit as delusory as the initial viewing — Aunty Boisjoly was fetching in a fur stole over an ivory silk evening number, lace *décolletée à volant,* and bold, black sash around the waist, closed with a silver scarab clasp. All she lacked was a menacing piano theme and a villain to tie her to the railway tracks. And yet, there she was, laughing loudly and touching Monty's forearm with an unmistakable 'oh, you' gesture. The key to the heart and happiness of Aunty Azalea, it would appear, was military heroism. I took in the object of her affection, bellowing some happy story about night-bombing, and I felt an affectionate, brotherly urge to sock him in the eye.

Barking quickly pulled the doors closed against the cold and menaced us all with his smouldering thurible of incense until we took our seats. Puckeridge joined Vickers, Alice and what had to have been a cook, and much gossiping ensued. Sally pinned her father between the end of a pew and the baptismal font. Cosmo was saving a seat for Everett across the aisle from Ivor, who sat on his own and blew his nose in a manner suggesting that he should remain so. Everyone was armed against the ambient temperature of the underfunded English church with woollens and scarves and convivial camaraderie. Barking had drawn thick velvet curtains over the transepts, and in time we couldn't even see our breath anymore.

Padget started proceedings with a fast-bowl directly from Stephen's Speech to the Sanhedrin and then delivered the surprise knuckle-ball of Paul's Inaction Before the Lapidation. All quite effective, if a little old-school.

"I can't tell you how moved I am to see so many of you here today of all days," announced Padget after the readings. "Our little community has been tried and tried hard during this festive season, and we have shown ourselves equal to the test. Miss Boisjoly..." Padget looked directly at her and she, amazingly, looked right back. "...Miss Azalea Boisjoly has not only come out, during a most difficult time, to observe this holy night with us but she's agreed to perform the accompaniment to the premiere of what I hope — and what I have been assured — will join the canon of English carols."

And sure enough, bookies would have been shooting themselves if they'd given odds, Aunty Azalea stood, gave a little bow to the congregation, and walked to the ageing upright piano which stood perpendicular to the altar.

"And her nephew, Mister Anthony Boisjoly, has agreed to sing for you my own composition, *Archdeacon Saint Stephen.*"

Applause exploded around me.

CHAPTER THIRTEEN

Whither Wanes
the Weather Vanes

Aunty Azalea was already reeling off a jazzy little mediaeval intro before the mists cleared and the intractability of my situation became clear. She must have committed us both to a show-stopper duet and I, in a dazzling display of deluded diplomacy, had doubled down.

I considered my options, from feigning a heart attack to actually having a heart attack, when I saw Aunty Azalea's girlish smile and mischievous squint, and her shoulders oscillating to the raucous harmony of *In dulci jubilo*. Perhaps I was going to make a fool of myself. Possibly I was about to offend the memory of the first Christian martyr. But what I was not going to do was disappoint my Aunty Azalea on this of all nights.

I joined her at the piano and withdrew from my pocket Padget's lyrics. A quick glance determined that they hadn't improved with age, and I was reminded that some of the words were blurred beyond recognition. I decided that the keenest strategy would be to cross that bridge when I came to it.

I knocked out the opening verse with few casualties.

"Famed far and wide for charity
Not to mention perspicacity
Saint Stephen spread the word of God
In a manner many found quite odd"

I scanned the audience and saw roughly what I expected. Even Soaky Mike was staring wide-eyed as though I'd just stood up in Saint Stephen's church of Graze Hill and read out the best bits of *Lady Chatterley's Lover*.

Aunty tapped out a little refrain, and I pushed out the chorus...

"So faithful was Saint Stephen he
When found accused of blasphemy
He looked up and saw the son of man
Standing at God's own right hand"

Those who are authorities in such matters say that if your audience isn't talking amongst themselves or in some other fashion distracted, you're doing well enough. By that measure, I was on theatrical fire, and the congregation regarded me with the solicitude with which I understand crowds in *Place de la Concorde* would gather round the guillotine during the later stages of the revolution.

Bolstered by this support, I gave full voice to the next verse...

"Saint Stephen was accu-u-used"

Looking ahead, though, I realised that I couldn't make out the last line.

"Quite falsely was abu-u-used"

I was rapidly approaching catastrophe, like a locomotive engineer at full tilt glancing casually up from his paperback to see that the bridge is out.

"He was dragged before the Sanhedrin..."

Rhymes with 'Sanhedrin', I thought. Vickers had something that would serve. What was it again? *Who proceeded to make fun of him?* No, not that. The closer I got to the last line, the further from my mind was Vickers' proposition, and for some reason all that remained as I reached the point of no return was what Ivor had suggested...

"For whom he played his mandolin."

Even Aunty Boisjoly raised an eyebrow. Soaky and Sally, Vickers and Puckeridge, and Cosmo and Everett looked at each other for confirmation that I had just reported that Saint Stephen, in his final moments, had entertained the jury with a few crowd favourites on the old lute. Ivor smiled broadly like a ninny who'd just been given some sort of lifetime ninnyship award. Padget pursed his lips and furrowed his brow and I allowed myself to fancy that he was trying to remember whether or not these were the words he'd written.

There was nothing to do but push on. I waded cautiously into the chorus, which passed largely without comment, and then the bit about Stephen facing the charges *unpertur-ur-urbed,* his soul, apparently, *undistur-ur-urbed,* and how his bearing was *ser-a-phic* and his face, by all accounts, *ang-el-ic.* I needed a stiff drink, and we weren't even to the bit about Abraham.

"Saint Stephen told the ta-a-ale
Of the origins of Isr-a-el
And unto all of them he said..."

And there we were again. What looks like a smudged thumbprint and rhymes with 'said'? Lots of things rhyme with 'said'. Dead... dread... someplace-else-instead. I had no time and no inspiration. At least the first time this happened I'd had Ivor's absurd, French-surrealist symbolism from which to draw. Now there was only Saint Stephen... the feast of Saint Stephen... Good King Wenceslas. I knew the moment it came to me that it was a mistake to pursue this stream of consciousness, because now all I could think of was Good King Wenceslas, tracking a peasant through a snowy wood, and telling his page...

"...In my footsteps thou must tread..."

...or something very like that. Nevertheless, it was an exponential improvement over 'For whom he played his mandolin' and only Padget seemed to notice the departure from the original libretto.

There's no need to list in detail the rest of the crimes against God and man that I committed that evening. Stephen had a vision, as we all know, which left the throng so *incensed* (which, happily, rhymes with *lack of evidence)* that they threw their coats at the feet of *Saul* (who, serendipitously, would come to be known as *Paul)*, and from there it only need be added that Padget's final couplet paired *atoned* with *stoned*, and our long, painful journey came to a merciful end with a tinkling little coda of Aunty Azalea's own improvisation.

T'was a silent night.

It was Ivor who broke the stillness with enthusiastic applause and, in an unexpected touch of mordant irony, he called for an encore.

Padget led us through a few dependable hymns and an homily on the theme of, I believe, honesty. Finally, he dished the wafers and wine and with a collective, convivial sigh of relief a cocktail party atmosphere prevailed in the nave.

I fell into conversation with Everett and Cosmo and we were soon joined by Barking, who had been collecting hymn books and extinguishing candles.

"Extraordinary performance, Anty," said Everett, shaking my hand and simultaneously incarcerating my elbow in a manner suggestive of all-in wrestling. "Remarkable. Are you a professional? Well, you should be. Transporting, that's the word. Like we were there, bearing witness as Saint Stephen was battered into martyrdom. I don't mind saying I was moved, Anty, truly moved. I think I might have cried a little. I mean, I didn't, of course, I'm not a little girl, but I might have."

"Couldn't have said it better myself, Anty," added Cosmo. "Particularly the chorus, the bit about the vision. How did it go again?"

"You know, I think I've forgotten."

Barking approached, then, with something of the demeanour of the dutiful sheepdog who's just noticed that it's past dinner time. "Yes, a very strong performance, Mister Boisjoly," he said in what I felt to be a somewhat perfunctory review of the recital. "I expect you'll want to be getting along, gentlemen. It's not getting any warmer out there."

"I say, Mister Barking, I meant to ask you something about the statue of Major Fleming," I said. Barking gave me one of those tight smiles that do the exact opposite thing that smiles are supposed to do.

"Oh, yes? What was that?"

"If it's not intruding on your artistic process, did Flaps ever sit for you?" I asked. "Or, more precisely, did you ever visit him at Tannery Lodge?"

Barking furrowed his brow, as though either trying to recall or wondering why I was asking such an obscure question when there was so much going home to be done. He looked from Cosmo, to Everett, and then to me. "Yes, of course. Several times. Twice. I think. Once, anyway. Why?"

"It's just that Cosmo here tells me that the place was lousy with war memorabilia — letters, medals, perhaps a captured German helmet with its spike ironically repurposed as a cigar punch. That sort of thing."

"Yes, that's right," confirmed Barking. "Most distracting, if I'm honest. Inevitably something would remind him of a story and we got very little actual sitting done."

"Once again, human conflict stands in the way of art," I sighed. "It's a wonder Michaelangelo ever got David to stand still long enough."

"Not going to stop you knocking together the memorial for a Spring unveiling, is it Trev?" contended Everett.

"Well..."

"Of course not," said Everett, and then added as a stage aside, "The man's a juggernaut. Nothing stops him when he snaps into action. Like a gale force. Wouldn't put it past him to smelt the bronze himself if the money runs out again."

"I don't suppose you noticed among the mementoes a complete set of the memoirs of Charles à Court Repington," I said to both Cosmo and Barking. "Roughly 621 pages per volume, handsomely bound with brass thingamabobs."

"I don't think so, no."

"No, well, I expect it wouldn't have stood out, much, among the field artillery and parade banners."

"What's all this about memorabilia?" asked Everett.

"It's been nicked," explained Cosmo.

"Let's say it's been moved, at some point, to parts unknown," I said. "I'd just like to get an idea of when that might have been. Do you recall the last time any of you saw Flaps?"

"Would have been the weekend prior," said Everett. "At the Cow."

There was convulsive nodding agreement to this and in that moment I noted that Soaky was in conversation with Mister Padget, leaving Sally free to indulge her passion for brooding in doorways. I excused myself and joined her.

"How's Hildy?" I asked, with carefully measured solicitousness — not too dispassionate, not too 'sorry I poisoned your cow.'

Sally, however, turned a warm, seasonal smile on me and said, "She's very well, now, thank you Mister Boisjoly. I'm sorry if I were a little short with you."

"Think nothing of it," I said and added, as backup, a cavalier wave of the hand.

"Lovely bit of singing, that. I expected two blokes dressed as a horse to trot across the stage, and I was all keyed up to shout 'he's behind you!'"

"There might be something to that," I said. "At first blush, you'd think it unlikely that the *Stoning of Saint Stephen* could take its place alongside *Dick Whittington and his cat*, but

I once saw a panto in Richmond which combined *Humpty Dumpty* with the story of Gunga Din. Queen Victoria was played by a giant hen."

"Is there nothing you can't get in London?"

"Actually, yes, there is," I said. "A drink at ten o'clock in the morning. Unlike the free citizens of the northern frontier, we're still subject to the Defence of the Realm Act, which compels us to drink at home until noon. I mean, if one wants a drink. Doubtless there are other things one can do while waiting for the pubs to open."

"It's the law here, too." Sally said this in a vague, let's-talk-about-something-elsey tone.

"Just not enforced, as such. Do you always open the pub at ten?"

"In the winter. If I didn't, no one would have anywhere to go at all."

"And it frees you to shut a bit early, too, doesn't it? And visit the dens of iniquity in that notorious hive of pleasure and vice, Steeple Herding."

"Do you not have any of your own business that you could mind?" asked Sally.

"Heaps. Don't get me started. I've been putting off a second fitting of a new set of opera tails since late October, and as we speak I'm neglecting my duties as Master of Handicaps at the Juniper Gentlemen's Club. Do you know it?"

"No."

"These are just examples, you understand, but family comes first," I said. "You can ask anyone — whenever an aunt of mine is accused of murder, I drop everything. I speak in general terms, you understand — the principle applies to any member of the extended Boisjoly clan, and all capital crimes."

"How do you know she didn't do it?" Sally steadied an analytical eye on my aunt, who was in that moment dangling freely off Monty's every word.

"Intuition," I replied. "Same way and to the same degree that you know Hildy didn't do it. What's more, I'm confident that some combination of knowables will prove that Aunty Boisjoly not only didn't do it, but couldn't have. For instance, the general consensus appears to be that the last time anyone saw the major, prior to yesterday, was the Saturday before."

"I already told you that."

"So you did. And how did he appear at the time?"

"Same as ever. Happy to talk your ear off and run up a bill."

"And yesterday?"

"Well, different. Like I told you, he paid off his cuff, made his goodbyes."

"A peculiarity which I have since confirmed, you'll be happy to know," I said. "What do you suppose happened?"

"No idea. He was fine when he first come in."

"He was, was he? Did you happen to notice the turning point?"

"I suppose it was sometime after that Montmorency bloke showed up." Sally gestured with her chin toward Monty, who appeared to be shouting and miming something about night vision to Mister Padget and Aunty Azalea.

"Monty wasn't in the pub when the major arrived?"

"He come in a few minutes later."

"And this was the first any of you had seen of him?"

"No, he was in on Christmas eve. Said that he just got to town. Asked about the major."

"I see," I said. "Most intriguing."

"Why?"

"Hm? Oh, it's a deducting thing. Difficult to explain to the layman," I said. "Who else was there that night?"

"Everyone, pretty much. Me and Soaky, Mister Barking, Mister Trimble, and that Millicent bloke, who says he's the major's nephew."

"And they all met Monty."

"Did they ever," said Sally. "Thought I was going to have to replaster the ceiling."

"Yes, Monty's is the sort of rich, resonant tenor best suited to the larger venues. East Anglia, say. No one else popped in? Constable Kimble didn't have to come by and put you under caution?"

"No, I closed up a bit early, in fact," said Sally. "When I come back from milking Hildy, Soaky had finished off the mulled wine by himself. He was trying to make another batch out of straight whisky and a half a stick of liquorice."

"Noted for future reference," I said.

"Right, that'll do, everyone." Barking accompanied this subtle proposal with gentle 'shove off' motions. The parties broke up and Padget established a checkpoint at the door. I joined the queue with the intention of exchanging a polite farewell but he once again grasped my hand. The vicar, as has been previously noted, was not a big man, but was surprisingly strong and bony, and the effect was not unlike catching my hand in a mousetrap.

"Thank you again, Mister Boisjoly, for raising my little oeuvre to such heights."

"Oh, well, you know, Vicar. One raises where one can. So long..."

"I wonder, Mister Boisjoly, if the slight modifications you affected were intended as permanent changes."

"If you like," I said, absently. "Consider them a gift."

"I'm particularly fascinated by the verse in which the archdeacon is brought before the Sanhedrin," Padget said, with a serious squint and a tone suggestive of the Gershwin brothers thrashing out the sequence of the overture medley. "It seemed a curious choice."

"What was?"

"You finished the verse with something about a mandolin."

"Was that not correct?"

"No, I mean, who's to say?" said Padget, philosophically. "But the original line was,

Who proceeded to make fun of him."

"Surely not."

"I beg your pardon?"

"I mean, are you quite sure that's not what I sang? Quite similar in rhythm, 'fun of him' and 'mandolin'. Easy to confuse the two, in the heat of battle."

An uneasy peace ensued while Padget furrowed his brow in dangerous reflection. I grasped for a distraction and, glancing back into the church, saw Monty escorting Aunty Azalea to the transept, presumably with the intention of revealing to her the wonders of the Graze Hill Museum.

"I say, Vicar," I said. "Do you recall when it was that you received Monty's letter, reserving a room?"

"Oh, yes, very clearly. We get so few letters. It was the third of the month."

"Plenty of time to hide the silver then," I said. "And when did he arrive?"

"Christmas eve," said Padget. "Just after tea. The station taxi brought him, so I assume that he arrived on the four-thirty from London."

"And he went directly to the Sulky Cow?"

"He did, as it happens. I offered to make another tea and show him the church, but he seemed eager to meet the locals."

"Drawn by the novelty of a strange metropolis," I explained. "I was like that the first time I went to Monte Carlo. And Cosmo? When did he first make landfall?"

"The beginning of November. We have a monthly arrangement." Padget said this distractedly, gazing off into the middle field, and I could see him silently mouthing something that rhymes with 'mandolin'.

"Must be awfully jolly, the three of you in the vicarage — the writer, the soldier, the man of the cloth. Sounds like solid grounds for a parable," I said. "Why do you suppose Monty didn't go visit his old war buddy immediately upon arrival?"

"I asked him that very question when we were walking back from the cow last night."

"I say, Vicar, you were at the pub last night? I understood you to be a beacon of temperance and an example to us all. To me, anyway."

"When I say the cow, I mean Hildy, the Graze Hill Golden."

"Ah, I don't blame you. We've met," I said. "Captivating conversationalist."

"I wished to consult with Sally Barnstable on a private matter, and I popped in when she was milking Hildy. I met Monty on the way home."

We were interrupted briefly by Barking, who stood in the middle of the nave, rattling the chain of his thurible and saying "Time, ladies and gentlemen, if you please."

"And what did he say?" I asked Padget.

"Say?"

"Monty. What did he say when you asked him why he hadn't yet been to visit the major?"

"Ah, yes. The major. Monty said that he wished to surprise him."

"Curiouser and curiouser. Did Flaps not know that Monty was coming?"

"I regret that I may have ruined the surprise. I mentioned it in passing to the major the Sunday prior." With this the vicar looked thoughtfully skyward. "I say, Mister Boisjoly, you don't suppose…"

"What is it, Mister Padget?"

"You don't suppose," resumed the vicar, newly inspired, "that there's room for a verse which elucidates the conversion of Paul. His name rhymes with so very many things."

Happily, in that moment, Monty shook foundations and traumatised infants for miles around with a mighty roar of "The ruddy cow is gone!"

I immediately formulated an internal plan to institute a search of all snowbanks in the region. Monty, however, was standing at the transept, holding back the curtain. Padget and I joined him there, along with Cosmo, Everett, Barking, and Ivor.

True enough, the purple velvet plinth was empty.

"Is something missing, Vicar?" asked Ivor through a much-travelled handkerchief.

"Nothing worth the attention of the police," said Padget. "Doubtless Mister Barking is in the midst of rearranging the museum. Isn't that right, Mister Barking?"

Barking replied with wide eyes and a stuttering denial.

"Me? No, of course not. Haven't I enough to do without playing museum curator, too?"

"Ah, well, doubtless it will turn up, Inspector," said Padget. "Good night, everyone. Don't forget, next Sunday is the Veneration of the Holy Family. By popular request, I will be repeating my free-verse defence of the authorship of the Johannine Epistles."

Ivor turned a weary eye on me.

"A tin cow, Inspector," I explained. "In the form of a weather vane. Not a tremendously useful device in a church transept, but an artefact close to the hearts of the honest villagers of Graze Hill."

"Is it valuable?"

"Can you put a price on heritage, Inspector? Can you measure birthright in pounds and pennies?" I asked. "Not really, no. It's a tin cow."

"Then why would anyone take it?"

"Jealousy? I doubt very much if Steeple Herding has any bovine weather vanes."

"If anyone was going to steal the weather vane, they'd have taken the bronze one off the clocktower," pointed out Everett. "Have you seen it Inspector? Glorious. Like a beacon of faith, shining out a message of prosperity for all of Hertfordshire and parts of Essex."

"I noticed it, yes," said Ivor with all the patience a man with a head cold shouldering the problem of a missing tin cow should have to muster. "I suggest we leave this mystery until morning."

This proposition inspired the always stirring scene of unanimous agreement, and finally we broke away from the relative comfort of an unheated church and into the Arctic wasteland that was Graze Hill Town Square, future site of the Flaps Fleming memorial bronze facsimile.

"Ah," boomed Monty, with hands on his hips and his gaze raised to the now brightly moonlit sky. "There it is."

We followed his line of sight to his line of reasoning. There, indeed, it was. The golden idol of the blasphemous cow was gone, and in its place was the tin original.

CHAPTER FOURTEEN

The Vanishing Visitor of the Solicitous Solicitor

"The intriguing question, of course, after how someone managed to steal a bronze weather vane from the clocktower, is why."

I made this bold contention from the forward-facing bench of the landau, as it jingled through the snow in the winding direction of Steeple Herding. The sun had dragged itself reluctantly from the gloom of a misty horizon, like a Wellington drawn slowly from a muddy furrow, and established a blurry presence in a murky midday sky. A chill fog lingered about us, and clung to bits to which it had no business clinging.

"The intriguing question, Mister Boisjoly, is why there was a golden calf on top of a church in the first place."

Ivor made this counterpoint from the other bench, his back to the wind and his shoulders enrobed in a horse blanket provided by Mister Barking, who was skillfully ho-ho-hoing us away from the constabulary.

"I concede the point," I said, munificently, for Ivor was not at his fighting best. "But you'll agree that it's of lesser pertinence to the mystery at hand."

"The mystery at hand is the murder of Major Aaron Fleming," Ivor enunciated nasally. "I'm having considerable difficulty bringing myself to give a hang and a half about the theft of a bronze weather vane."

"No, I confess, that when you weigh them against one another, murder does on the face of it appear to be the graver of the two offences. But surely you're as captivated as I am by the uncanny similarity of the crimes."

Ivor rocked with the gentle motion of the sleigh and regarded me beneath hooded eyes, as one awaiting elucidation or on the cusp of falling asleep.

"Well?"

"I refer, of course, to the fact that both the murder of Major Fleming and the theft of the bronze cow are, at first glance, impossible," I explained. "Major Fleming was seen alive hours after my aunt discovered his body. There is no question of anyone mistaking the time, because she visited Tannery Lodge before sunrise. And yet, hours later, in the fullness of morning, he walked into the Sulky Cow, and stood everyone a round of drinks."

"Easily explained — your aunt is lying."

"There you go," I declared. "Impossible. And then we have the theft of the weather vane and the reinstallation of the original tin version. Possibly someone could have climbed the clocktower, but every suspect was in the church when it happened."

"Also easily explained — that's not when it happened. It

171

was done at some point during the day, or the night before."

"I think I would have noticed."

"Would you have?" asked Ivor. "Can you swear that you saw the bronze weather vane during the day yesterday?"

On reflection, I realised that Ivor was correct. I certainly took note of the monstrosity when I first encountered it — it was impossible not to — but it's extraordinary what extremes the human mind can come to regard as commonplace. I couldn't say that I would have noticed had the cow been exchanged within the last twenty-four hours, and I said as much to Ivor.

"And I asked Mister Barking," continued Ivor, "he couldn't say for certain when he last saw the tin cow in the museum. He closed the curtain the night before."

"Ah, but what about the footsteps in the snow?" I asked.

"What footsteps in the snow?"

"Exactly," I said. "There were none. The snow on the roof of the church was entirely undisturbed. Returning us once again to the same, single, inescapable explanation for both mysteries."

"Which is?"

"Ghosts," I said, rather unnecessarily, in my view, but Ivor's intellect was oppressed by a head cold, which reminded me... "That reminds me. I brought you a present." I withdrew from my overcoat a smoked-glass flagon. "The French call it *sirop contre la toux*, or *cognac*, in the vernacular. Two generous helpings of this with hot water and, before you know it, you'll be breathing freely and debating the limitations of a free press in a democratic society."

Ivor received the bottle with a touching desperation, and

folded it into his coat.

"Ho ho ho. Ho," declared Barking, and his giant Clydesdale replied with an assenting "P-p-p-p-puh."

"Steeple Herding, gentlemen."

"Thank you, Mister Barking," I said. "Where are we going, Inspector?"

"Solicitor by the name of Josilyn Boodle."

"Solicitor by the name of Josilyn Boodle, Mister Barking," I said. "If you could kindly direct us."

"Steeple Herding has a solicitor?"

"Not only that, Mister Barking, but he goes by the singular name of Josilyn Boodle, if the inspector's sources are to be believed. I'm as astonished as you are."

"You could ask at the post office."

"We'll do just that, Mister Barking. I expect you have an empire to build or a market to conquer, so if you could get all that out of the way in time to pick us up around two, you'll find us in..." I scanned the doughy, snowy, main street of Steeple Herding. "...that pub."

"I'm not going into any public house in Steeple Herding."

"No, and I wouldn't ask you to, any more than I'd ask a Capulet to pop down to a Montague off-licence. I'll keep an eye out for you."

A crinkle-eyed postal elf with a bow tie and spring link sleeve garters gave us very precise directions to the home office of Mister Boodle, and Ivor and I were soon at the door of a handsome *maison de maître* of the sort that Harley Street doctors are forever hiding behind brass plaques. This house had opted for a more modest iron sign with raised letters spelling "Josilyn Boodle, Solicitor".

"I'm sure I don't need to remind you, Mister Boisjoly, that you're here as a courtesy." Ivor reminded me, apparently feeling the need to do so nevertheless, and then tapped the door knocker. "You're not to say a word, unless I explicitly ask your opinion, is that understood?"

"Couldn't be clearer, Inspector, even if your cold didn't give you the elocution of a man being smothered by a pillow. Feel free to call upon me to translate, if the need arises."

The door opened exactly as far as needed to reveal the aquiline features of a patrician woman with an extremely judgemental eyebrow.

"Yes?" she asked, pointedly and, I daresay for the season, a bit piquishly.

"Inspector Wittersham, Scotland Yard, to see Mister Josilyn Boodle." Ivor managed to combine imperious and weary into the same tone, which caused whatever he said to carry an implied 'or am I going to have to nick someone?'

The door swung open on a smart hallway that divided home and office in exactly the same way that Constable Kimble had failed to do. The right-side wall was wainscotting to roughly the height of wainscotting, and frighteningly domestic wallpaper with cornflowers or lavender or some such the rest of the way up. On the left was a plain, white wall with a black lacquered door. The letter-opener-shaped woman marched us through the office door, which led to a pleasant waiting room with two deep, worn-leather divans on either side of a bay window looking out onto the snowy street from whence we had just come.

"My husband doesn't often see visitors in this office," announced the woman who in that instant came to be known to us as Mrs Boodle. "He normally receives clients in his

London office." She said 'London' the way people in London say 'Kensington' and people in 'Kensington' say 'Buckingham Palace'. "I'll tell him you're here." She slipped through the crack in the door and was gone.

Ivor slumped sideways on a divan like a prima donna in a death scene, and I sunk into the other and flipped through a small stack of tracts on various themes of law, such as *A Passion for Probate*, by Seward Braith-Wairing, FBA, and *A Practitioner's Guide to Trespass and Poaching*, by Federick-Anne Damby-Squires, KC and KCSI. Spoilt for choice, I nevertheless selected *Copyright Infringement and Remedy*, partially because there were a dozen copies, and partially because it was authored by none other than Josilyn M Boodle, Solicitor, London and Environs. It was a simple, folded, stunningly dull treatise with a picture of a serious-minded Boodle on the front, taking a dim view of something that was occurring to the left of the photograper.

In the photograph, he was a handsome, clean-shaven, professorial type, an image which was entirely undermined a moment later when the door burst open and the real Josilyn Boodle clattered in. Since the photograph was taken he'd acquired a thin moustache and lost a monocle, and he'd developed a sense of *joie de vivre* that appeared largely absent among the legal essayists of Great Britain, if these brochures were anything to go by.

"Allo, allo," sang Boodle. "Which of you is the rozzers?"

"Inspector Wittersham," said Ivor, rising like a flag of mourning. "This is Mister Boisjoly."

"Boisjoly, eh?" Boodle shook our hands enthusiastically. "Any relation to Azalea Boisjoly?"

"My aunt," I explained, and stopped there, to avoid

destabilising the delicate balance of the police interrogation.

"I know her. I know of her, I should say." Boodle opened the other black lacquered door in the waiting room and led us into his dark grotto of an office. There were heavy curtains on the window at the back, a low desk lamp, and a sense of oppression which was compounded by bookcases which had us completely surrounded. Boodle sat behind his desk and we took two high-backed, black leather visitors' chairs that swallowed us the way a jellyfish swallows a prawn.

"Tea? Coffee? Something a little more festive? I think I've still got about a hundred bottles of whisky remaining from the annual Christmas tradition observed by Londoners who, every year, try to introduce their legal counsel to the boundless delights of chronic alcoholism."

"Thank you, no," said Ivor, and I was forced to mirror this rash refusal with a reluctant gesture of despair. There's no thirst, I've long ago discovered, like the thirst of one refusing a drink against his will.

"Right ho," said Boodle, and fixed Ivor with a pose not dissimilar to that which he flashed for the cover of his seminal treatise on copyright law. "What can I do for Scotland Yard?"

"I regret to have to inform you that Major Aaron Fleming is deceased."

"Oh. I... see." Boodle concentrated for a moment on his hands. "That's rather rotten news, isn't it? How did it happen?"

"The major was murdered," said Ivor. "I understand that he was your client."

"Yes. Yes, he was. Murdered, you say? Do they... do you

know who did it?"

"An arrest is due imminently," said Ivor. I objected to this, of course, but with an immense exercise of will kept my views to myself. I had no control, however, over what had become in the few moments that had felt like hours, a clawing thirst. I coughed lightly, and Ivor received it as a breach of conditions. He issued a sidelong reminder to maintain my neutrality.

"In the meantime," continued Ivor, "if you could enlarge on the nature of the business that you had with the major."

"I was his solicitor. He had rather a lot of administrative details that needed seeing to — he received rents and tithes on most of the farmland in Steeple Herding and Graze Hill."

"And you collected these payments on his behalf."

"In a nutshell."

"What becomes of all this money?"

"Bank, mainly." Boodle raised his palms and shoulders in the helpless shrug of creativity constrained — the purebred legal racing horse yoked to the plough of mundane financial transactions. "The major didn't have a great deal of interest in his legacy, as such. Instead, he had a pathological fear of debt, and instructed me to take no risks with his money."

"Had he cause to worry?"

"Not even a little," said Boodle. "He came back from the war to a very stable income and virtually no outgoings. As did I — I inherited the Fleming trust from my father on return from service."

"Were you also a pilot, Mister Boodle?"

"Me? Oh-my-dear-no," laughed Boodle. "Colour-blind, myopic, and prone to motion sickness. I was also too tall, which surprised me rather, and I have all the spatial-awareness of a clam, which didn't. No, I saw action as quarter bloke, blighty division. Got to France first week of September, 1914, got home second week of September, same year."

"Wounded?" guessed Ivor.

"Deeply." Boodle nodded gravely at the painful past. "They took my rifle away when I accidentally discharged it in mess hall. It was a dreadful overreaction — the sergeant got his hearing back in time. But they said a man of my talents would contribute more from Dover. Can't say they're wrong, but my survivor's guilt gave me nightmares for, oh, must have been a good week. Sure you won't have a drink?"

Boodle sprung from his office chair and deftly manipulated volume four of *English Tort Law*, which swung open, along with volumes one through three, to reveal an ingeniously equipped library bar. He splashed the perfect quantity of brown happiness into a thick glass, then held up a tantalising bottle and gave it an inviting shake.

"Thank you, no," repeated Ivor, with what I took to be deliberate spite.

I cleared my throat, subtly and discreetly, like a man of breeding dying in the desert.

"Did you wish to add something, Mister Boisjoly?" asked Ivor at last.

"Well, as it happens..." I began, my eye on volumes one through four of *English Tort Law*.

"Oh, yes," bulldozed Ivor. "Mister Boisjoly was asking about the status of the rights to the major's life."

"Rights?" Boodle took a long, luxurious draw on his drink

and leaned back in his chair. "You mean, as in story rights, books and whatnot?"

"And motion pictures, for instance."

"Is this regarding the mad plan of the chap claiming to be his nephew?"

"That's right."

"Well, Flaps was a public figure. There are no special rights required to tell his story, unless you want your biography to enjoy the dubious distinction of being 'authorised', or, of course, you're planning on defaming him."

"Defaming?"

"The great risk in selling someone else's story is, should they object to any of it, and they can show in court that you've done harm to their reputation or earning ability, they can drive you to ruin. Moral is, if you must make a picture about a war hero, best wait until he's dead."

"I say, Mister Boodle, in your waiting room I noticed an article authored by you on the subject of copyright law. Does it cover what you just told us, about defamation and the deceased?" I asked.

"Briefly. The real meat of the piece though is in derivative works and summary remedies. Would you care for a copy? I have hundreds."

"I'll pick one up on the way out."

"If we could return to the subject of the death of Major Fleming," steered Ivor.

A shadow crossed Boodle's face. "You're quite sure you know who did it?"

"Quite sure," said Ivor.

"Well, some of us are more sure than others, who are merely sure who didn't do it," I clarified.

"Mister Boisjoly, I wonder if you might pop across to the pub and keep a watch for Mister Barking," said Ivor with calm reproach. Or so he thought, because what he didn't know was that across the street at the pub is exactly where I wanted to be.

"You can count on me, Inspector," I said. "No Barkings will get past my ceaseless vigil. Pleasure meeting you, Mister Boodle."

I let myself out into the waiting room where Mrs Boodle was restacking the legal treatises that I had carefully left in disarray.

"I say, Mrs Solicitor," I said. "One gets the distinct impression that the real brains of this operation, as is so often the case, is the lady of the manor. Is it correct to assume that you handle your husband's appointments?"

"Those here in town, yes," she responded, unfolding like a jackknife.

"Did Major Aaron Fleming come round very much, would you say?"

"No," said Mrs Boodle. "Mister Boodle would visit him in his home, in Graze Hill. He never came here."

"To his immense loss, I'm sure," I said. "What about his nephew, Cosmo Millicent?"

"Why, no, or, rather, yes."

"I understand. I've met him myself, but I am going to have to ask you to pick a side."

"He was here this morning," she said in hushed wonder, as though Cosmo's appearance alone carried a hint of scandal, but by morning light he was a positive outrage. "But this was his first visit and, I should think, his last."

"Quite possible," I agreed. "He's a man of mystery. But why do you say so?"

"He just disappeared," she said. "He asked to see Mister Boodle, without an appointment, which is an exception one typically only makes for the police, of course. He insisted, so I put him in the waiting room. I went to tell Mister Boodle that he was here but while I was going up the stairs Mister Millicent dashed out the front door. He didn't even bother to close it."

"Doubtless intimidated by the rarified atmosphere of British Law," I explained. "I often feel quite nonplussed when I'm up before a magistrate at Bow Street."

"Are you a barrister, Mister Boisjoly?"

"No. I know rather a lot of barristers, but typically when I'm before a magistrate it's in my capacity as a private citizen."

"Does this happen often?" Mrs Boodle's eyebrows condemned me quietly.

"I suppose that depends very much on your definition of often," I said. "I thank you for your time, madame, I'll impose upon it no longer. If you need me, I'll be at the Steer & Steeple, across the street."

The Steer & Steeple was a jolly, warm, deep-stained oak and red-carpet pub of beamed ceilings and a crackling fire and laughing, apple-cheeked patrons. It was fully tooled-up with whisky-and-warm-waters and nooks by the window from which to study the fascinating discipline of copyright law and watch for the arrival of either Barking or Ivor or both.

Ivor won by a length and, after visiting the bar to order, of the vast array of options, tea, he joined me at the window.

"That was certainly illuminating," said Ivor, hugging himself into the upholstery.

"I'll say," I agreed, brandishing as an illustrative prop my copy of *Copyright Infringement and Remedy*. "There's a bit here that should interest you very much. Did you know that according to the terms of the *Norman Costumal*, which forms part of the basis of our modern libel laws, one who falsely accuses another of being a 'manslayer' must not only pay damages but must also, in a public place no less, hold his nose with his fingers and declare himself a liar. You'll want to watch your step, Inspector."

"I think I'm on safe enough ground," Ivor said, and then added, "Thank you," as the barman slid a tea tray onto the table. "After you left we got onto the subject of Major Fleming's last will and testament."

"You're not going to tell me he left the lot to my aunt."

"No, not at all." Ivor paused to sip his tea with loud satisfaction. "Didn't even have a will, it turns out."

"Then what is it that gives you this disagreeable and entirely uncharacteristic air of smug self-satisfaction, may I ask?"

"The major didn't have a will because he didn't need one. Just before he died, he signed over all his worldly possessions to your aunt."

CHAPTER FIFTEEN
Devious Dealings Over Dunkirk

Aunty Boisjoly was in the library, performing a pagan fertility dance and strewing flowers from her hat. Those weren't her precise actions, but she was humming, and by the standards of Aunty Boisjoly, open humming approached the naked abandon that would secure most people a choice room with a view of the lawns of Bethlem sanctuary.

"Just a word of advice from one with better than average familiarity with the view from the dock," I said, choosing my words delicately, "you might want to avoid chirping like a madwoman when the King's Counsel asks you to characterise your reaction to the brutal murder of your former lover."

"Please don't speak in riddles, Anthony," said Aunty, pirouetting on her heel away from the fire. "It gives you airs, like those fellows with unkempt beards who smoke small cigarettes and pronounce on things from the recesses of a Paris café. Fix me a drink."

My sixth sense had already drawn me to the sideboard, whereon I found machines and makings necessary for the composition of two generous whisky-sodas.

"That's very rich indeed, coming from one of England's foremost contortionists. Tell us your methods, Miss Boisjoly, are you of the Classical School? Or do you subscribe more to the Stanislavski Technique, and go about telling little fibs whenever the opportunity presents itself?"

"What are you babbling about, Anthony?" Aunty accepted her drink and swirled it distractedly as she wandered back to the window.

"Do you deny that you denied your romantic entanglement with Flaps Fleming?" I asked. "I'll warn you, before you answer, that there's unimpeachable testimony to the contrary. I'm not naming names, but you should know that the witness for the prosecution is a respected country clergyman with a dangerously extensive familiarity with the Book of Acts."

"Ah."

"The *mot juste*," I agreed. "Ah."

"I wasn't fibbing, Anthony. Flaps ended our engagement before he died."

"Well he could hardly have done so afterwards, could he?" I pointed out. "Surely you see how this looks."

"It's why I didn't tell you."

"No, it's why you didn't tell the police," I said. "Your motives for not telling your adoring nephew defy reason. What happened?"

"It was just before Christmas. I would always pop by Tannery Lodge for a natter, every evening. It's been our little arrangement for months now. But just a few days before Christmas he was very cold and circumspect, and said that he thought that he would soon be leaving Graze Hill."

"Did he say why?"

Aunty nodded uncertainly. "He said that he was done hiding away from life. That it was time to rejoin the world." Her eyes twinkled with dewy sadness. "He said I would hold him back, Anthony." And the dew overflowed.

"Rather harsh. Are you aware that days before his death the major went to his solicitor to transfer title of all his holdings to you?"

Aunty Azalea shifted gears abruptly. "All of it?" She wiped away the tears. "Blimey."

"My thoughts exactly. You didn't know, then."

"I didn't."

"Pity," I said. "Quite sure? Because it rather dilutes your motive for murder if you did. Not entirely, of course, but you're less likely to kill someone who's just given you a fortune than, say, someone who hasn't."

"Quite sure."

"Well, can't be helped. Anything else you're keeping from me? You don't have a secret sideline spiriting nobles out of revolutionary France?"

"No, that's everything."

"I'm relieved to hear it." I swallowed my drink and put the glass on the tray. "Inspector Wittersham will be anxious to know your views on your newfound fortune, and I'm afraid you'll have to be more forthcoming, in future."

"Oh, Anthony, that inspector's not coming back, is he?"

"Not in the near term, no," I assured her. "He has a head cold, and I took the liberty of lifting a 1925 Ragnauc from your cellar. It has a pleasantly floral nose with traces of wheatfield harvest, and the bouquet finishes with hints of fruit and almond, neatly masking an alcohol content that could float a barge. I don't expect to see him again until late tomorrow afternoon."

"Very wily, Anthony. Now if you can only suggest a way of getting you out of the house for the evening, I could enjoy dinner alone with Monty."

"Say no more, Aunty," I said. "I'll have Vickers shovel something onto a tray and bring it to my room, and then I'll unleash my newfound expertise in copyright law on the regulars at the Sulky Cow."

Sun sets in the wintertime in Hertfordshire around tea time, after which all sense of time and space is absorbed by the twilight and fog. There was a dreamlike quality to the evening, if one is unfortunate enough to have dreams which are not only foggy and cold but also clammy and wet. The warm, dry, glowing interior of the Sulky Cow, therefore, was particularly welcome and welcoming when I clattered in.

The scene was set exactly as it had been when I first laid eyes on the place — Sally was at her counter, performing one of those infinite tasks that always seem to be in the purview of barkeeping, Barking and Everett were in unidirectional conference at a table, and the familiar stack of coats next to the fire turned out to be Soaky Mike, marking the inexorable passing of time by chewing on an orange rind from the bottom of his cup of mulled wine.

"Evening gentlemen." I ladled myself a cup of steaming stupefaction and took up space on the upholstery between Barking and Soaky. "Cosmo not in tonight?"

"Poor chap's head down working on his book," said Everett. "I admire that, I don't mind who knows it. Wish I could write. Probably my greatest regret, among legion others. Just don't have the gift, like he has. Got about enough economy of language to order a pint. After that I'm dumb as a teak tortoise."

"You saw him today, then."

Everett nodded briskly. "Only for a second. He was stoked on pure, anthracite inspiration. Says that your performance last night gave him an idea for a cracking ending. The man's a juggernaut. A powerhouse. It's humbling, downright humbling, to be in the presence of crackling creative energy."

"He didn't say anything about securing the rights to tell the major's story?"

"Not to me. Say anything to you, Trev?" Everett directed this to Barking, who was eyeing the clock, which in that moment ticked over to a perfectly perpendicular nine o'clock, and Soaky snapped into action and helped himself to a cup of cheer.

"Eh? Oh, no, not that I recall." Barking had allowed his mind to wander, and when it returned it appeared to have stumbled on something and knocked it over. "Said he might be back in later."

In that very moment the door flew open as though struck by a cannonball, bounced off the bench and slammed shut again. A second effort was made, followed by a staggering inspector from Scotland Yard.

Ivor counted several coins onto the counter, saying, "A cup of this mulled wine of which I have heard such excellent reports, Landlady, and a round for my friends."

"Good evening, Inspector," I said. "You seem much improved."

"Thanks to you, Mister Boisjoly, and the fine people of France." Ivor occupied a stool across from me at our table.

"Nothing for a cold like an *eau de vie* from the Cognac region," I declared. "The prescribed posology though, as a rule, is to combine the brandy with hot water and an absorbing novel featuring soldiers and/or consulting detectives."

"Ran out," explained Ivor.

"You drank the entire bottle?"

"You didn't say not to."

"No, fair enough. You have me there," I conceded. "I also neglected to advise against breaking a hole in the ice and having a bathe in the canal, so I'll mention it now, in case you get the urge."

"To France," said Ivor, and raised his cup. We all joined him in toasting, but a moment later Ivor lowered his cup and examined it suspiciously.

"Did I drink that already?"

"You neglected to fill it." I leapt to ladle duty. "Allow me."

"Off-duty, Inspector?" asked Everett.

"I'm never off-duty. Why do you ask?"

"I admire that, Inspector. It's part of what makes me proud to be British, the thin blue line. Ever vigilant, never flag nor fail. I just thought you had it all sorted out, is all."

"Not quite," admitted Ivor. "I like to be thorough. And I'm still bothered by the footprints in the snow."

"Constable Kimble says that they prove conclusively that Miss Boisjoly — begging your pardon, Anty — must have done the murder."

"The murder? Pish." Ivor rather exaggerated the 'shhh' on 'pish', as though he was slowly deflating. "That's all done but the gavelling."

"Then what is it about the footprints, Inspector, which still weighs upon your mind?" I asked.

"It's as you said — there should be footprints on the roof of the church. Unless..." Ivor held my eye while he took another draw on his hot humour. "Unless it happened before yesterday's snowfall. Then the tracks would have been covered up, at least enough to hide them from view."

"You're talking about the missing cow," I surmised.

"Wouldn't we all have noticed it missing sometime during the day?" asked Everett.

"The inspector's view is that, hardened as our minds are to the sight of the calf, we didn't take note of the fact that it had been replaced." I explained.

"Most ingenious, Inspector," said Everett. "How do you proceed from here?"

"Good... old... fashioned..." Ivor tapped the table with each word, more or less. "Police work. I mean to search the museum."

"What? Tonight?" I asked.

Ivor squinted in thought, as though focusing on the question, which occupied an uncertain spot somewhere in the air between us. "Yes. Why not? I'm feeling particularly..." He looked into his cup for inspiration. "...intuitive tonight."

"It's too late," complained Barking, nodding toward the

clock. "It's just gone nine-thirty."

"Crime never rests, Mister Barking," declared Ivor.

"I'll have to get the key from the vicar," said Barking, with petulant resignation. He disentangled himself from behind the table. "Back as soon as I can, that's assuming I can even raise Mister Padget at this time of night."

Barking wrapped himself against the cold and left us.

"Good lad," said Ivor.

"Solid gold," agreed Everett. "However, I feel quite confident, Inspector, that you'll find no evidence of foul play in the museum."

"Why do you say that?" Ivor asked this distractedly, then drained his cup and held it out for a refill, and I obliged.

Everett took an uncharacteristically prolonged breath before declaring, "I believe that the bronze Hildy was taken by none other than... the Graze Hill Ghost."

"There's a Graze Hill Ghost?" I asked.

"I think so," nodded Everett thoughtfully. "Do you like it? I find the alliteration works well. Having said that, there's a lot to be said for 'The Spirit of Hertfordshire'. Broader appeal, more upbeat and modern, puts Graze Hill at the centre of a regional campaign."

"Would this be the ghost of Flaps Fleming, who visited the bar?" I asked. "Or the mischievous phantom who nicked the bronze weather vane?"

"Both. All of them. Including the spirit squadron. Have you heard that story? It's a cracking tale."

"I did. Did you hear it from the major?"

"Monty told me," said Everett. "You could hear a pin

drop. The major never mentioned it, though. Too painful. You could tell by the look on the poor man's face. Monty kept asking him if he remembered the names of the fallen. It was all the major could do to look him in the eye."

"But the major wasn't shy about any of his other stories, up to and including the encounter with the Zeppelins, when the entire squadron, according to Flaps, lost their lives."

"Chilling. Still sends shivers down my spine."

"I've seen this before," said Ivor, as though confiding an insight. "He's endeavouring to make a point."

"Very astute, Inspector. I am. Everett, did the major ever tell you about emerging from a cloud in perfect formation with a squadron of enemy fighters?"

"An extraordinary tale of iron will," confirmed Everett. "Do you think you could have held your nerve in such an encounter? I doubt I could have, but that's the difference between heroes and the rest of us. No doubt Saint George was much the same, finding himself in close quarters with a dragon."

"How could a pilot, even a very skilled fighter pilot, survive an encounter with a full complement of experienced bosch assassins?" I mused.

"By being English," posited Everett.

"Hear hear," added Ivor. The men clinked their cups together and drank deeply.

"And what was the point of the ghost story?" I asked. "It's obviously piffle, so why tell it? And why tell it so publicly in the presence of one ostensibly able to put the lie to it?"

"Embellishment, Anty," explained Everett. "Among the finest British traditions, dating back to Milton. There's a chap who knew that truth in the telling of lies is like meat in the making of pies — excellent if you happen to have some on hand, but if you're going to maintain interest you're going to want to tart it up a bit."

"Exactly," I agreed. "Monty was making a point. A very risky, dangerous point."

"And what point are you trying to make, Boisjoly?" asked Ivor.

"We had it backwards, Inspector. We believed the first person who told us about the double agent in the squadron," I said. "But Monty wasn't the spy — Flaps was."

"Steady on, Anty."

"The ghost story was Monty's way of taunting Flaps with the names of the dead. And it's why he's here — for revenge."

"Where's Monty now?" asked Ivor.

"At Herding House," I said, rising and pulling on my coat. "Alone, with my aunt."

CHAPTER SIXTEEN

Tense Dark Work in a Dense Dark Wood

I left brisk instructions with Sally, whom I judged the most reliably likely to be in contact with a giant policeman before the night was through, to send Kimble along at his earliest possible convenience.

The night struck a discordant tone with full, flossy, flitting snowflakes falling in profusion, forming a close crowd that managed to be simultaneously sinister and convivial, like a society wedding. I pushed on against the elements, feeling decidedly heroic and fancying I looked much as Jack London must have pictured the character Buck when he wrote *The Call of the Wild*.

I'm not sure what I expected when I burst through the door of Herding House but I feel sure that it wasn't empty silence. The door had been left unlocked. The lights were out in the foyer. I inched through the darkness until I could delicately, carefully, give the dinner gong a wallop that, on a cricket pitch, would have been good for three runs. Four if there was long grass.

Within moments the lights came up and Puckeridge appeared, somehow looking every bit the butler in spite of a silk dressing gown with an elephant embroidered on it.

"Sorry to drag you away from what looks must have been a rollicking great knees-up in the Sultan's tent," I said, "but Herding House is still unfamiliar to me and I don't know where one goes, exactly, when one needs urgently to burst through a door shouting 'ah-ha!' Could you direct me?"

"I beg your pardon, sir?"

"Where are Aunty Azalea and Monty?"

"Miss Boisjoly and the Flight-Lieutenant have gone for a late-evening walk, sir. In the woods, I believe."

"Muster the staff, Puckeridge, we must find them. Have you any torches?"

"I'm afraid not, sir."

"Pitchforks?"

"No."

"No matter," I said, without fully meaning it. "I'm running on ahead."

"Is anything the matter, sir?"

"I hope not, Puckeridge," I said, pulling open the door. "I truly do. See you on the moors."

The snow swirled about me as though I was, for the whipping winds and searching cold, a matter of great interest. I trudged through the snow between Herding House and Tannery Lodge, following two sets of footprints and a single set of walking-stick-prints, all of which were quickly filling in. The tracks led me to the treeline and deep enough into the woods to become convincingly lost. After that, the trail was swallowed by the arctic snows.

In the depth of the woods the wind whistled through the trees and I experienced that special variety of disorientation available exclusively on winter nights in dense forests. Nevertheless, I forged ahead, squinting against the thick snowfall and, for all I could tell, walking in a circle. After somewhere between five and twenty-five minutes, I finally reached the treeline again, but I could only assume that I was on the wrong side of the woods from the village, for before me white hills rolled away into the murky horizon. I sighed at them, though in retrospect I realise they were blameless, and turned back into the darkness of the mystical wood in which East was West and Tops was Turvy. I reasoned that if I managed to walk in a straight-ish line, I would be heading toward the village and hence executing a scientific sweep — modesty forbids, but someone else might employ the term 'military precision' — the most likely to flush out Monty before he strangled Aunty Azalea or made good his escape under cover of the storm.

Sure enough, after pushing through snowdrifts the approximate size and density of the sand dunes of Namibia, I saw the silhouettes of two figures projected onto the screen of the swirling snow. They blurred at the edges and presented a bit like a Chinese shadow theatre with even less plot than those sorts of productions usually have. This one appeared to be about two chaps standing in the driving snow, idly chatting about this and that, but then the story picked up a bit when one of the shadows quite suddenly stabbed the other in the neck with an immense knife.

"Ack!" I yelled, or something very like that. I was probably aiming for an authoritative 'Halt!' or plaintive 'Noooo!' but — and I'd only just discovered this myself — I'm not at my creative best when witnessing a murder. Nevertheless, the effect was roughly as expected — whatever I managed to shout, it was received as 'If you're done murdering that fellow, perhaps you'd care to step this way and do me, next.' And that's what he did.

Or at any rate, that was clearly his intention. I had something quite different in mind, and I dashed off into the night. My plan, if it could be called a plan and not merely a series of rapidly overleaping feral impulses, was to employ my unique familiarity with the terrain and qualities of the storm to once again trace a circle, luring the assailant into the dense, dark forest, and doubling back to see if there was anything that could be done for his victim.

I didn't look behind me but the only sound to join the howling wind and my own fumbling footsteps was someone else's fumbling footsteps, and so I felt confident that the 'luring' part of my plan, at least, was highly effective. I ran on, neither gaining nor losing ground, and then, drawing inspiration from raw fear, I dodged sharply right and behind a tree. I stopped and listened. The pursuing footsteps continued, briefly, and then were lost to the winds. Cautiously, bent low, I worked my way back to the scene of the crime.

Cosmo was beyond help. I'm no expert but I can say with some confidence that, at the very least, it was quick. His eyes were open and he looked, quite understandably, surprised.

The wind ebbed briefly and the curtain of snow parted long enough for me to see that we were at the treeline, and just beyond that was the village. I could make out no buildings over the ample accumulation of snow at the woods' edge, but I could clearly see the clocktower — Cosmo had died at five minutes after ten.

And, if his killer had his way, my own death would be recorded some minutes later. I couldn't see him, but I heard the snow crunching under his footfalls as he figured out my cunning plan and was now following my footprints. I noticed that the knife that had been used to dispatch Cosmo was gone, doubtless still in the skilful hands of his assassin. I looked around quickly for a weapon or cover or, actually this should have been top of the list, Constable Kimble, and saw only the high snowbanks that had gathered at the treeline.

In two strides, I was diving through the air, and I sunk neatly and fully into the soft snow. Doubtless something stuck out, but it was dark and this was my best chance. I listened to the footsteps as they slowed and came to a stop next to Cosmo's body. I imagined the killer examining my footprints which, to him, would appear to have ended where I began my Olympian stride into the snowbank. His first instinct would have been to look up to see if I'd climbed a tree. Realising that was a ridiculous idea, he'd reach the next logical conclusion — I was hiding.

His footfalls were slow, soft and searching. They shuffled from left to right, stopping at each checkpoint, doubtless to listen for the chattering of teeth or knocking of knees. Nevertheless, he was getting nearer. Through the wall of snow and howling wind it was difficult to determine distance, but some combination of sound, instinct and primal dread gave his position at, approximately, right in front of me, seconds from seeing me, and one second more than that from driving his blade through the snow and into my thumping heart.

It felt like hours passed, but I think that I was holding my breath so, realistically, probably not. Still there was no sound. In my mind's eye he stood there, just the other side of a flimsy film of snow. His blade, having developed a taste for human blood, flashed hungrily in the moonlight. I decided to give it a little longer. Not such a bad place to be, a snowbank, all things considered. Not the most comfortable place I've ever spent an evening, but certainly by a wide margin the most agreeable conditions in which, to date, I'd ever waited out a homicidal maniac.

Gradually, reason resumed its reign. Some indeterminable period of time had passed, and a quick inventory determined that I was still alive. It was possible that the killer was waiting me out, but it was much more probable that he'd elected to cut his losses rather than risk being found next to a bleeding corpse. Furthermore, while it was far from a primary concern, by this time a considerable portion of the snowbank had melted through my clothing, and in addition to shivering with fear I was shivering for the standard reasons. I decided to take a peek.

The moment I determined that I was alone — apart from poor Cosmo, of course, who was still very much a presence — I was overwhelmed with cold and damp. I followed the treeline, merely as a precaution, until I could see the Sulky Cow. Steeling my nerves, I crept out of the woods and across open land.

I ached with cold. Everything I wore was wet and it conducted and compounded the cold in a way that was only marginally less comfortable than facing the elements naked. I yearned for the warmth of the pub and even more so for the hot, healing potion that even now simmered in an iron pot on the chimney hook.

The pub was closed. Locked tight and dark. I looked back at the clocktower — midnight. I had been hiding in a snowbank for nearly two hours, and now I faced a cold, wet, aching, quaking walk to Herding House.

I'm still not entirely sure what the poets mean when they claim that a heart 'sings', but when I saw Herding House, glowing warm and welcoming at the windows and the front doors thrown open, and Aunty Azalea standing at the foyer wrapped in blankets and fretting for her nephew, *somebody* was belting out Handel's *Hallelujah Chorus*. I staggered inside and into the arms of the blood relation, and wrapped myself in homecoming.

"I have taken the liberty of running you a bath, sir," said Vickers, whom until then I hadn't noticed. "I'll just warm it up, sir, and lay out fresh evening wear."

"Momentarily, Vickers. Aunty, we must rouse Puckeridge and send him to fetch the constable — there's been another murder."

"The constable's here, dear," said Aunty. "So is the inspector. They're in the drawing room."

And indeed they were. Kimble was leaning on the mantelpiece with a cup and saucer, and Ivor was sitting in a Bergère chair with a snifter of brandy and his feet on a matching ottoman, gazing dreamily at the flames. Next to him was Monty, molesting the fire with a poker and splashing about a snifter of his own.

"Well this is all very cosy," I protested. Then to Kimble I said, "Did you not receive my urgent request to aid me in my search for... him... and... yes, I see the situation for myself, now."

"Miss Barnstable conveyed your message, yes sir," said Kimble. "But by then Miss Boisjoly and Flight-Lieutenant Hern-Fowler were in the Sulky Cow."

"It was all very convivial," said Ivor. "You should have been there. Everybody else was."

"Well, I can tell you who wasn't," I said. "Cosmo Millicent."

"Chinless chap with a lisp?"

"That's him, yes."

"He was there."

I looked for confirmation to the sober policeman.

"Mister Millicent was in the pub."

"Along with everyone else? Including Aunty Azalea?"

"Yes, sir," said Kimble.

"Excellent," I said. "In that case, Constable, you don't know it yet but you're hot on the heels of a serial killer — when did Cosmo Millicent leave the pub, and who else left at the same time?"

"He left when we all did, sir — quarter of eleven."

"Quarter of eleven?" I asked. "Hang on, when you say, quarter of eleven, do you mean to say one quarter of the hour of eleven, meaning fifteen minutes after ten, or quarter to eleven? Not that it makes the slightest difference, because that can't be correct in either case — Cosmo Millicent was murdered tonight at five minutes past ten."

"If that's so, Mister Boisjoly," said Kimble, "then tonight the Sulky Cow was visited by another ghost."

CHAPTER SEVENTEEN

Six Sinister Secrets

"I shall never be warm again, Vickers." I made this statement of bald fact under the weight of two down-filled duvets, accompanied by an extensive private collection of hot water bottles.

Vickers was throwing back the curtains, freeing a steely winter daylight to establish a beachhead in the Heath Room.

"I have brought tea, sir," said Vickers. We both looked around the room in a moment of anticipatory silence. "I have neglected to bring tea, sir," added Vickers. "I'll rectify it immediately."

"Tea is unequal to the task at hand," I said. "Draw me a scalding bath, and keep the boiling water coming. Then have my mail forwarded to the bathroom."

"I regret, sir, that you have visitors. Inspector Wittersham and Constable Kimble are in the drawing room."

"Of course they are," I lamented. "What time is it Vickers?"

Again we both looked around the room. Even I, on arrival in dairy country, had adopted the native custom of not winding my watch nor remembering where I put it. Vickers looked out the window.

"Just past first milking, sir," he concluded.

"That explains it. How is the inspector looking, by the way?"

"Decidedly green, sir."

"I'll just bet he is," I said. "He was self-medicated to the gills last night. Very well, Vickers, please inform our guests that I shall be down shortly."

Puckeridge was rebuilding the ruins of a late, light breakfast of eggs, bangers, blood pudding, *épinard au beurre, crêpes au caramel,* and an enormous clay urn of coffee poised over a chafing dish on an ingenious tripod. Kimble appeared to have composed a personalised breakfast roll of everything but the crêpes, inside a crêpe. Ivor was by the fire, sipping a cup of coffee and, by all appearances, trying to focus on a spot somewhere in St Albans.

"What ho, forces of law and order," I sang as I fell upon the scene. "Give me a moment to impose my favourite of the deadly sins on this sideboard before we delight in the details of last night's gruesome slaughter. Blood pudding, Inspector? There are a couple of specimens that look particularly well-congealed."

Ivor closed his eyes and when he opened them again, some considerable time later, he was squinting at me as though I was an uncomfortably bright light source. I took my plate to the writing desk and tucked in.

"Did you find Cosmo roughly as I left him, Constable?" I asked.

"Mister Millicent was indeed the victim of a violent attack," confirmed Kimble. "He would have died instantly."

"I suppose there's some comfort in that. Any luck with the crime scene? Did the killer drop his wallet or carve his initials into a tree?"

"There was only the body of the victim. Any evidence, such as footprints, were long prior obscured by heavy snowfall."

"Yes, I noticed that. I could barely see a thing. I'm afraid that my account will be of little use except, as I mentioned, with regards the time of death. I assure you that the clocktower was quite unequivocal — it was five minutes past ten."

"You couldn't identify the killer nor, for that matter, the victim, until you were face-to-face," observed Ivor pettishly, "but you could read the clock some... what was it, Constable, five hundred feet away?"

"Closer to eight hundred."

"Eight hundred feet, in driving snow, and you could read the clock."

"It sounds improbable," I said, "until you account for wind conditions. The snow was whipping in squalls, randomly opening and closing lines of vision. My view of the clocktower was brief but unmistakable."

"So was ours," said Ivor. "I had call to look at the clock when we left the pub. It was ten forty-five, and Mister Millicent was with us and, to my very strong recollection, alive."

"I'm curious what drew your eye to the clocktower."

"You'll recall that Mister Barking went to fetch the key

to the church from Mister Padget. He came back, some time later, and said that the vicar didn't answer. But then, perhaps fifteen minutes after that, Millicent and Padget himself joined us in the pub. I found that suspicious, and took note of the time as we left, with respect to Mister Barking's claim that it had been too late to raise the vicar."

"How very curious," I agreed. "Tell me, Inspector, if you were able to make out the clock, why do you find it so unlikely that I could?"

"The pub gives out practically in front of the church."

"Yes, by about eight hundred feet."

"I can confirm the time, Mister Boisjoly," said Kimble. "The clock in the pub and the clock on the church both read ten forty-five when we left. You must have been mistaken."

"And yet, I'm not," I mused. "Most peculiar. In fact, not most peculiar — not even a candidate for most peculiar, out of three impossible crimes in as many days. Something else strikes me as notable about your account of last night's festivities at the Sulky Cow — my aunt was among those present."

"Apparently Hern-Fowler goaded her into coming," explained Ivor. "Must have decided, at the last minute, not to kill her to prevent her from exposing him as a spy."

"Yes, I suppose I may have been partially wrong about that," I confessed. "But only partially. How did they seem?"

"Loud," said Ivor. "But your aunt took to the pub like a child takes to a circus. Sudden wealth and freedom from personal commitment appears to have liberated her spirit."

"Very coyly put, Inspector."

"I confess it was quite disarming, seeing someone

experience a pub for the first time," said Ivor. "It never occurred to me that anyone might not know what a beer tap was for."

"Talking of which, I understand that Mister Padget's presence in the Sulky Cow was something of a novelty as well."

"Millicent brought him," said the Inspector. "He was very keen about his plans for his book, and was harassing everyone to recall what they could of Major Fleming's stories."

"Did he say what fired this fresh new shoot of productivity?" I asked.

"He seemed to know that his copyright issues had been sorted," said Ivor. "And he said that he had already written the ending... thanks to you, now I think of it."

"That's the second time I've heard that. Everett claims that my improvisation of Mister Padget's Christmas carol inspired Cosmo to new heights of creative output, with specific regard to the epilogue. Do you suppose he thought he figured out who killed the major?"

"We know who killed the major."

"Indulge me anyway, Inspector. Unless you've also figured out with ruthless certainty who stole the golden calf and who murdered Cosmo Millicent."

"Very well," sighed Ivor. "Do you recall the words to the carol?"

"Thankfully, no, not very well."

"Could it have been that bit when Saint Stephen told the Sanhedrin to follow in his footsteps?"

"I sang that?"

"You did." Ivor nodded solemnly, as though confirming

some abiding tragedy. "That couldn't have been in the original version, surely."

"You'd be surprised, Inspector. But no, I expect you're right — I probably invented that bit."

"Perhaps Millicent had some theory about the footprints in the snow," proposed Ivor. "Constable, is it possible someone else visited Tannery Lodge, walking in the major's impressions in the snow to disguise his own?"

"No, of course not," said Kimble. "Have you ever tried that? It's almost impossible for a few steps, never mind all the way from the Sulky Cow, over the hill, to the lodge, and back again. I examined the footprints carefully — they were made by one man."

"At any rate," I added in a supporting role, "it doesn't change the fact that Aunty Boisjoly discovered the body hours before the major supposedly made those tracks."

"Assuming she's telling the truth."

"I confess, I am proceeding under that assumption," I said. "Indeed, the key to all three mysteries is that Aunty Boisjoly is the only one who isn't hiding a secret."

Winter in Hertfordshire can be a fluffy, crisp, shimmering, blue and white celebration of the anticipation of the glad return of Persephone to the realm of living, planting, growing and harvesting. It can also be a bleak, grey, endless twilight of dark clouds and penetrating cold. This particular afternoon gave not a fraction of a whit for the return of Persephone.

I slid and crunched and tripped and cursed down the hill toward the village. Vickers had swaddled me in long underwear and flannels, a wool greatcoat and a mohair scarf composed of the hair of at least a dozen moes, and yet in my very marrow the memory of my time in the snowbank persisted like a war wound.

While, coincidentally, musing on the subject of war wounds, I spotted Monty wobbling toward me up the hill. He was deftly employing his walking stick to put the ice in its place, and he hailed me like he recognised my colours across Portsmouth Harbour.

"Hallo, Boisjoly."

"Good afternoon, Monty," I tenored back, and we slid to a stop. "Visiting my aunt? Again? People will start to talk. Although, in light of everything else that's happened in the last three days, I can't imagine what they'd find to say."

"Remarkable woman, your aunt, Mister Boisjoly. Did you know she'd never been in a pub before last night?"

"I'd always assumed," I said. "Tell me, Monty, do you recall what time it was when you left the Sulky Cow last night?"

Monty nodded confidently. "Twenty-two forty-five on the button."

"And was Cosmo Millicent among the throng?"

"Everyone was there. Apart from you, of course."

"You all went your separate ways, I suppose."

"Hard to say, actually." Monty looked back toward the Sulky Cow as a visual aid. "Some lingered. Visibility was poor, on account of heavy snowfall. Why do you ask?"

"Oh, just making conversation, as one does," I said. "Seeking common ground on, say, the weather, the lively, iconoclastic Graze Hill social scene, the brutal murder of Cosmo Millicent. Read any good books, lately?"

"Poor chap."

"Indeed. Where did you go from the pub?"

"I took Azalea home, and then she sent me back out into the storm."

"Did she?" I asked. "But you were there when I arrived last night."

"I mean to say, she asked me to go looking for you," explained Monty. "I didn't find you."

"I appreciate the effort exactly as much as if you had," I claimed. "Did you see anyone else out enjoying the winter evening?"

"Not a soul."

"No, of course not," I said. "What about Christmas Eve, when you first arrived in Graze Hill? I understand that you visited the Sulky Cow."

"I did."

"But not your old wingman."

"I wanted my arrival to be a surprise."

"So I understand," I said. "It's what you told Mister Padget, as you walked home with him that evening, in the company of Cosmo Millicent."

"I believe so." Monty regarded me with a circumspectful squint. "Why do you ask?"

"Why does one ask anything, Monty?" I asked. "To hear the answer. Can we count on you for cocktails tonight?"

"I expect so."

"Excellent. Puckeridge has a case of *Veuve Clicquot* '23 on ice, you won't want to miss that, and later I'll be revealing your secret."

The Sulky Cow glowed weakly in the gloom, compared to its usual warm, receptive blush. Sally was behind the bar and, in contrast to her normally industrious approach to her vocation, she was drinking a whisky straight. She nodded shortly as I came in, but expressed neither grief nor glee in seeing me. Everett was at a table, alone, with a tankard of something about which he appeared to have forgotten, in favour of the study of some bewildering notion that floated before him.

The fire was a dwindling stack of orange embers, and there was no iron pot on the chimney hook.

"I'm sure I'm not the first to point this out, Miss Barnstable," I said. "Someone's nicked your mulled wine. Has Hildy been in?"

"Season's over, Mister Boisjoly. I can heat you up a teapot of muscatel, if you like."

"I'd rather sleep in a snowbank, on balance," I said. "Just a whisky, as it comes. You don't know where Mister Barking is, do you?"

"At the church. He's taking down the weather vane."

Sally poured a generous glass of cask-aged barley juice, and I leaned conspiratorially near.

"Do you recall what time you pushed the orphans out into the cold last night, Miss Barnstable?"

"Must have been about quarter of eleven," she said. "Just after Constable Kimble come round to remind us of closing time."

"Rather late for you, isn't it?"

209

"Like I said, the season's over. It's back to normal hours of operation."

"Where did you go afterwards?"

"Where did I go?" she replied with surprise. "I looked in on Hildy and then went home. Why do you ask?"

"I assume you know what happened last night."

"You think I had something to do with that?"

"In a word, yes," I said. "I do think you had something to do with that. You see, Miss Barnstable, I figured out your secret."

"That a fact?" she said, less as a question and more as a sound to make while affecting to be distracted by a stain on the bar.

"'Tis. Want to know how I did it?"

"I'm sure I couldn't care less." Sally spoke distantly, conserving her energies for the invisible stain. "You can tell me if you like, I'm not troubled either way."

"Then you won't mind waiting until tonight, say, cocktail hour, at Herding House."

"Got the pub to mind, don't I?"

"That won't be a problem, Miss Barnstable — everyone will be there."

I positioned my whisky and myself squarely in Everett's line of vision.

"Oh, hullo, Anty," he said, noticing me with a start, followed in quick succession by his pint, from which he took an unsatisfying swallow.

"What ho, Everett," I said. "I hope you won't mind me observing that you're not your usual voltaic self. Batteries low?"

"Just a little distracted, I suppose. It's all rather a blow, this."

"Of course. Terrible tragedy."

"I say, Anty." Everett had what appeared to be a flash of inspiration. He leaned across the table toward me. "That carol of Padget's — is it true that you made up a lot of that yourself?"

"Just the bits that made sense."

"Well, then, there we are..." Everett was picking up speed, like a freshly cranked gramophone. "*You* can write it."

"I can write what?"

"Call it what you like. I wouldn't presume to suggest, but if you're at a loss for a title, you could do worse than *The Hero of Graze Hill.*"

"Are you talking about Cosmo's book?"

"I'd say it belongs to all of us, in a way."

"You want me to write it?"

"It's what he would have wanted," Everett pronounced solemnly. "And he'd have wanted you to be right quick about it, too. The reading public soon forgets these moments of drama. We don't seize the moment, there'll be another foreign skirmish or some American flying a hot air balloon to the moon or someplace, and Flaps Fleming will be forgotten. Let us allow Cosmo Millicent to die for that for which he lived — to tell the story of the Hero of Graze Hill."

"I take your point. There's almost no value at all in two brutal murders if the subsequent sensation can't be spun into gold. I'm not sure I'm the artist for the art though, in this case, Everett. I specialise in the shorter work — eulogies, rash proposals of marriage, that type of thing."

"Treat it as you see fit. A series of vignettes, for instance — air battle, air battle, love interest, air battle, couple of stories of Flaps' childhood — that should probably go at the beginning, but you'd have a free hand."

"A free hand, you say."

"It's the only way. Mind like yours. Needs to soar like an eagle. Float on the vagaries of poetic inspiration."

"There might be something to that — and I could write the conclusion that eluded Cosmo."

"There you go," enthused Everett then, downshifting, said, "What conclusion?"

"Who killed Flaps Fleming, and how," I said. "Make a topping ending, don't you think? Although it'll rather limit the directions in which one could take a sequel."

"You know who killed Flaps Fleming?" Everett lowered his voice and raised his expectations. "Who?"

"You wouldn't prefer to wait and read the book?"

"Just a clue."

"I'll tell you all, Everett, tonight, over cocktails, at Herding House. You and everyone else."

"Everyone?"

"Only fair — I'll be divulging everyone's secret, including yours."

Just as my sources had informed me, Barking was balanced on the top third of a complex ladder formation from the ground to the church roof, then to the clocktower, and finally to the dizzying heights at which weather vanes become practical. As I arrived, the tin Hildy slipped her foundations and tipped into his hands.

"You might want to stand back a bit, Mister Boisjoly," Barking called down to me. "Or take refuge inside the church."

"Right oh, Mister Barking. You going to be long? I was hoping for a word."

"Depends very much on how long I need to spend up here on top of this ladder in sub-zero winds having a chat about how long I'm going to be, Mister Boisjoly."

"Message received, Mister Barking. I'm off to church."

As I passed through the open doors of the church the tin cow was received by the snow with a dead thud. The snow caught it in a solid grip, no bounce, right-side up, so Hildy's tin head was peeking above the surface with a sanguine, resigned countenance, as though she knew this was bound to happen, sooner or later.

Padget was vicaring about the front of the church with candles and hymnals and the like. When he saw me he set down his burdens and approached me like I was a bird that had been rejected by its mother.

"Why, Mister Boisjoly, what brings you out today of all days?"

"Seeking sanctuary from the storm," I said. "There's a rather larger than usual number of tin cows falling from the sky this afternoon."

"I mean to say, I heard about your ordeal last night. It must have been frightful."

"Worse for Cosmo."

"Poor, poor Mister Millicent," agreed Padget. "Who could have done such a thing?"

"Perhaps more tellingly, when could someone have done such a thing?"

"I beg your pardon?"

"Do you recall what time you left the pub last night?"

Padget reflected. "I believe it was after ten-thirty. The constable came in then and reminded us that it was closing time."

"And you and Cosmo came and left together, is that right?"

"Yes, that's right," said Padget, but then, upon brief reflection, amended his statement. "We all left together, but I returned home alone. Mister Millicent said that he had some business to arrange with someone."

"I don't suppose he mentioned who, did he?"

"I regret not."

"No matter, Mister Padget," I said. "But for a few stylish flourishes, the case is all but closed."

"That's a tremendous relief. Has Inspector Wittersham solved both murders?"

"I doubt that very much," I said. "I did. The turning point was when I realised that everyone in Graze Hill is harbouring a secret, and those secrets have managed to combine themselves into the perfect cover for murder."

"You don't mean that."

"I don't, actually, I mean to say the *nearly* perfect cover for murder. If I could figure it out, almost any over-educated fundi with heightened observation skills probably could. If you'd care to learn how, you'll want to be at Herding House this evening at the cocktail hour."

"Surely, though, you don't mean to imply that everyone in Graze Hill has a guilty secret."

"That's exactly what I mean to imply, Mister Padget, and what's more, I know what they are — even yours."

Barking was standing in the snow with a forlorn sort of patina to his map, as though musing bleakly on how his lot came to be so tightly entwined with the tin cow industry.

"Can I be of any assistance with that, Mister Barking?" I asked.

"I'll be getting the sleigh to bring it back to the smithy, thank you, Mister Boisjoly."

"Heavy, is it?"

"More awkward than heavy — it's hollow on the inside, but it's still a weather vane in the shape of a cow."

"What about its successor to the clocktower? That looked quite substantial."

"Oh, that was heavy." Barking nodded weightily. "Solid bronze."

"Any idea how it was done?" I asked. "Exchanging the bronze cow for its tin predecessor? They'd have had to not only spirit this one out of the museum without anyone noticing, but climb the roof, as you've just done, but without using ladders nor leaving tracks."

"No idea — and it's not for lack of thinking on it. Have you had any thoughts?" asked Barking.

"Me? Oh, yes, I know how it was done, and what's more, I know why."

"You do? Really?"

"I do," I confessed with the coy modesty for which I'm widely known. "If you'll join us this evening at Herding House you can be there when I divulge every detail, including your dark secret."

CHAPTER EIGHTEEN
Astray and Adrift in a Drift

Puckeridge was at his post to release me from the grip of a cold and unforgiving afternoon and into a warm and forbearing Herding House. I took the opportunity to pose some searching questions.

"Tell me something, Puckers, and feel free to speak your mind — if I were to say to you, 'I know your secret', how would you respond?"

"I expect that I would ask to which secret you refer, sir."

"Jolly good answer, Puckeridge," I said. "So would I. Well, have no fear, to me you remain a sublime enigma."

"I'm most gratified to hear it, sir."

"I do have a follow-up question, though, if it's not too personal — do we have any dried fruit in the house?"

"Doubtless something could be found, sir. Have you any further specifications apart from it being dried and fruit?"

"I'm not particular. Candied apricots, currants, or even the humble raisin will do nicely," I said. "How about cinnamon?"

"Miss Boisjoly is fond of a *cannelle râpée* on her porridge."

"Is she now?" I said. "She's a woman of hidden depths, is my aunt. Finally I'll need a young-ish Merlot or Cabernet-Sauvignon. Or, rather, you will. We're going to be requiring an economy-sized pot of mulled wine. Four bottles should be plenty, so make it eight."

"Very good sir."

I settled the programme for the evening with Puckeridge, from whom I learned that Ivor was still on the premises, asleep by the fire. I therefore noiselessly skulked to the drawing room and gently coaxed him awake with the soft crash of a heavy pewter salver allowed to flutter gingerly onto a granite hearth from about shoulder height. He was as amenable to my plan as could be expected of a man with a morning-after head like a damp cricket pitch on the sixth day of a five-day test.

The last and most vital part of my strategy lay ahead — I retired to the Heath Room and hardened the sinews with a carefully mixed tincture of Scottish craftsmanship and the legal minimum of soda water.

At the cocktail gong, some hours later, dressed and fortified for an evening's entertainment, I danced down the stairs to the foyer, where Puckeridge stood sentry at the door.

"Everything as arranged, Puckeridge?" I asked.

"All but the guests, sir."

"Not a one?"

"Only Miss Boisjoly is in the drawing room, sir."

"Well, early days," I contended. "Beguile my aunt with

stories of your tempestuous youth, will you, while I call order to the proceedings."

Evening had stolen the hour and the steely mist of morning had hardened, thickened and finally broken into giant snowflakes which joined forces to form even more giant snowflakes. As I made the familiar journey to the Sulky Cow they fell from above like a slow, soft bombing raid, obscuring the night in a billowy haze and filling in my tracks as quickly as I made them.

The pub door was locked, which corresponded with expectations, and so I continued deeper into the village until I encountered Soaky Mike, alone, standing point duty at the entrance to Hildy's little *pied à terre*.

"Good evening Mike," I called. "Have you seen, just as an example, anyone at all?"

"Off in the woods, ain't they?"

"I don't know, ain't they?"

"Arum," confirmed Soaky Mike with a grim nod. "Hildy's gone missing."

"What? When? Where?"

"After last milking, into the woods. That's why everyone's gone looking for her."

"Well, this is monstrous. Why would she do such a thing and, perhaps more within the immediate scope of affairs, how do we know she went into the woods?"

"Tracks," said Mike, nodding at the freshly installed layer of undisturbed snow. "They're gone, now."

"So I see. And you're left here, in case she returns."

"Arum."

"And to keep you from being left alone in the pub."

"Arum" Soaky repeated, this time with much pathos.

"I'll join the search party then." I took my leave with high strides through the deep snow, calling back, "Listen carefully for my signal, it strongly resembles the sound of a little girl crying for help."

Employing the exact strategy which failed to get me killed the night before, I endeavoured to navigate a straight line through the woods. Conditions were similar, too — the night was dark, the flurries were dense, the snow of the forest floor was deep, and I was sharing the woods with a murderer.

At what I optimistically estimated to be midpoint between the village and the other side of the wood, my left foot found a tangle of undergrowth that it liked, and I fell face-first into the snow, like a tin cow falling off a clocktower. There's a reflex that follows falling on one's face that, no matter how remote and isolated the events, causes one to look about to see if anyone's laughing. In that moment I heard a footfall — a crunch in the snow and the snapping of a twig — which was all perfectly normal but for what followed. Nothing followed. A footfall in a dark wood followed by silence suggested, at least to me in my heightened awareness of the fragility of life, that I was being clandestinely pursued.

"Soaky?" I called, remembering the last time this had happened. The reply was again the unmistakable sound of nothing at all, apart from the wind whistling through the trees and putting a wicked backspin on the snowflakes as they fell. I lay in the snow, listening to this eerie accompaniment, and then eased to my feet. Beneath me the snow squeaked, as very cold snow will, although my particular tract managed to trumpet across the land like an air-raid siren.

The only thing for it was to continue into the deep wood and, intermittently, stop and listen. Sure enough, I caught out the sound of someone failing to follow my rhythm. I tried the diplomatic approach, but there was no reply to my friendly "Hallo?" and several nonchalant calls of "Oh, well, I guess there's no one there after all, is there Constable Kimble? You probably won't be requiring that shotgun, then."

By and by, an unearthly glow emerged between the trees before me, and I knew that I was approaching the barren, undiscovered other side of the wood. I'd feel safer, I knew, once out in the open, but as I approached the forest edge the wind dropped off subtly, exposing the muffled sounds of someone manoeuvring into position between myself and open country. The noises were little more than the shifting of snow and scraping of undergrowth, but to me they painted a vivid picture of an axe-wielding maniac, raising his weapon with mighty arms like tree trunks, held in hands the size of prize-winning yams.

I crouched and crab-walked a path parallel to the treeline. Finally, I could see a massive silhouette, contrasted against the grim twilight.

"Hildy," I said and she turned on me an expression of existential woe. "What are you doing out here at this time of night? We're missing cocktail hour."

The elements had swept enormous dunes against the treeline and Hildy had found one of the most intractable and stuck right in. She was deeply embedded to the point of bearing an uncanny resemblance to her effigy where it fell into the snow in front of the church.

"I'll bet you're just wishing I'd thought to bring the shovel. I don't blame you, I'm wishing the same thing myself, but I will point out that you're in no position to criticise."

In what appeared for only a short, happy, moment, to be a coincidence, Hildy and I heard a distinctly shovely sound, as of a ploughshare sinking into yielding earth, and we squinted into the darkness.

"Stand by," I whispered. "We're about to be joined by a murderer."

Presently, a figure came into view. At first it was just a shadow cast against the swirling curtain of snow. It was made larger-than-life by layers of wool and fur, and it carried a shovel over its shoulder like an axe, as it stepped into focus.

"Everett," I cried. "What exceptionally good fortune. And you've brought the shovel. Very foresightful."

Everett stepped closer and then stopped. He smiled the cold, self-satisfied smile of the man who has explicitly not come to dig cows out of snowbanks.

"I'd propose working from the other side," I said, gesturing toward the wall of snow, a good eight feet high, that separated us from the open meadow beyond. "I'll stay here and comfort Hildy. Or, if you'd prefer, I'll do the spadework. I have some on-the-job experience."

"You couldn't just leave it alone, could you?" said Everett. "Everything had neatly arranged itself — beyond all expectations, I might add. All details neatly slotted into place. Two nice, clean murders, no suspicion on me at all, done and sorted, and then you have to upset the works."

"I say, I am sorry," I said. "Perhaps if you'd spoken up. Or, if that wasn't practical, and I can see how it might not have been, you might have chosen a different scapegoat than my Aunty Boisjoly. We have a code, we Boisjolys, when it comes to fitting our aunts up for murder."

"I didn't choose her, did I?" said Everett, visibly annoyed by my line of reasoning. "It was all happenstance, pure good fortune. The tracks in the snow, the time of the deaths..."

"I know, Everett. It was clear to me the moment I saw the scene of the first murder that I was looking for an impetuous, improvisational killer. It's why I suspected you from the start."

"You never suspected me."

"I did," I counterclaimed. "In a single breath you address a dozen subjects, and they're all superlative. You're incapable of nuance, so I imagine you must have worshipped your father as a giant among men. He should have been the hero, shouldn't he, Everett? And not the man you hold responsible for his death."

"He would have been legendary." Everett looked skyward at this, and his eyes glistened. "They'd have built statues to him in Trafalgar Square."

"Instead, as a novel treatment for survivor's guilt, he walked into a propellor."

"Because Flaps Fleming wouldn't let him fly."

"Keen eyesight does seem rather a fundamental prerequisite for the job," I pointed out.

"There was nothing wrong with my father's eyesight," insisted Everett. "Flaps couldn't bear to share the glory — he knew that my father would have been the greatest fighter pilot in the entire flying corps. The entire war. The entire history of war."

"I suppose that's a good enough justification as any for cold-blooded murder," I said. "And then when Cosmo figured out how you got away with it, you had to kill him too, once again profiting from an extraordinary confluence of circumstance to appear to be in two places at once."

"Cosmo Millicent didn't figure out a thing. I expect I could have confessed to him and he'd still have needed a diagram."

"I daresay you're right," I said. "Nevertheless, he discovered something that, if made known, would prove that you were the only one who could have killed Flaps Fleming. I realised it, too, and have since told the police."

"No you haven't." Everett said this with a disturbing confidence. He also raised the shovel and advanced menacingly.

"No, you're right," I confessed. "I haven't. But they know, anyway."

"How?"

"A lot of bother might have been avoided if you'd just followed this simple advice from the start, Everett — think it through. How did you find me this evening?"

"I followed you," he said. "I knew that when Hildy went missing you'd join the search, and I'd have you exactly where I wanted you. And now if you'll just hold that position..."

"In a moment, Everett. I knew that your impetuous nature would induce you to seize what you saw as yet another convenient opportunity for murder, and your compulsion to monopolise the conversation would cause you to confess. That's why I had Puckeridge lure Hildy to the edge of the forest with a pot of mulled wine, for which she has a pronounced weakness."

"You're lying."

"I wish I were," I said. "But we have to face the fact that Hildy is a slave to drink. We believe, though, that with time and compassion..."

"Shut up, Boisjoly, I've heard enough."

"I think we all have," I said, backing away and finding myself blocked by the snowbank. "You can come out now, I think, Inspector."

For the briefest of instances I saw what Everett might have looked like if he weren't the most recklessly self-assured man in England. His face fell. The weight of the shovel dropped onto his shoulder. His eyes searched the woods and the wall of snow. In due course, though, as Ivor continued to fail to present himself and I whiled away the moments reflecting on regrettable things I did as a child, the concrete certitude returned to Everett's bearing.

I doubt that with a year's specialist training I could reproduce the dodge that saved me from the first swing, which whistled just above my shoulders. I had by then exhausted whatever talent I had for late-night-forest-shovel-jousting, and on the backswing Everett caught me square on the bean. I must have spun at least a hundred and eighty degrees because my next sensation was of lying face-down in the snow. I rolled onto my back just as Everett raised the shovel like a spear, and then time seemed to slow, and henceforth unfold at an inexorable, protracted pace.

The blade of the shovel descended. It was a singularly

fascinating movement, and I felt as though I could watch it for hours, but that I couldn't possibly move out of the way. Simultaneously, with a howl like a Scottish infantry regiment, Hildy broke free of the snowbank. She leapt up and over like a thoroughbred steeplechaser, and bounded toward Everett, catching him just above the cummerbund on her stubby, heroic horns.

It was then that time returned to its midseason stride and provided the gratifying image of Everett reversing through the air as though struck by a cannonball, to come to rest against a tree with a satisfying 'thock'.

"All right, Boisjoly?" Ivor's disembodied voice drifted to us on the wind.

"Where are you, Inspector?"

"Other side of this snowdrift. I've been looking for a way over."

"I certainly hope that you heard Everett's confession, Inspector. I very much doubt if I could contrive to get him to repeat it."

I might have heard a deep sigh. It might have been the wind.

"Yes, Mister Boisjoly, I heard it."

CHAPTER NINETEEN

The Seriously Circuitous Solution

Puckeridge was in his element. He conducted Vickers, the kitchen maid, the cook, Alice and Henry, the boot and knife boy, as though they composed all he needed to mount a full and final assault on Amiens. Champagne corks popped, plates clattered, silver service clanged, syphons fizzed, and a great iron cauldron of mulled wine sloshed on the hearth. Next to the fire, as per my personal request, stood the Christmas tree of Flaps Fleming.

The drawing room was cosy and congested with more guests than it had seen in Aunty Boisjoly's entire tenure. Ivor, Sally, Soaky Mike, Barking, Padget, Monty and Aunt Azalea chattered and laughed and gossiped with that inimitable, irreproducible spirit of camaraderie that comes at the end of a period of intense, immense distrust. The overwhelming consensus appeared to be that, if one of them had to be a murderer, it was just as well it turned out to be Everett Trimble.

"Another hot cup of hearth and holly, Inspector?" I offered, drawing the ladle from the steaming pot.

"I will, thank you Mister Boisjoly, and I'll raise it to you." I filled his cup and, good as his word, he raised it. "I was convinced that your previous success was purely a matter of local knowledge and fleeting luck," he said. "I confess now, willingly and sincerely, I didn't expect it to last this long."

"I return the toast, Inspector, in honour of your talent for faint praise," I said. "But I admit, there was a bit of luck — once I realised how it was done, it was obvious only one person could have done it."

"Of course." Ivor tapped his cup to mine and drank deeply. Conversation waned, then, and an anticipatory silence reigned.

"All right, then, Boisjoly, tell us how it was done," said Ivor at last.

"How which was done?" I asked. "The murder of Flaps Fleming, hours before he appeared to his friends at the Sulky Cow? The stealthy, acrobatic, and impossible swap of the bronze weather vane? Or the killing of Cosmo Millicent, before my eyes, while he was with all of you at the pub?"

"I think all of them, perhaps, in your own time."

"Very well," I said. I distributed more mulled wine and took a speaker's position before the fire. "Let us begin at the end, with the death of poor Cosmo Millicent. Of course, Mister Barking already knows how Cosmo managed to be drinking in the pub while simultaneously being stabbed in the forest, and I think I should assume that, had they known they were hindering a police investigation, he and

Miss Barnstable would have spoken up."

Sally and Barking looked at each other and then found their hands or shoes more distracting.

"You'll recall that everyone confirmed that the clocktower, when you left the pub in the company of Cosmo Millicent, read ten forty-five, even though when I looked at it, just after he'd been killed, it displayed five past ten. The explanation is simple — you were all wrong. Mister Padget happened to mention to me that the clock, like many other unwanted gifts to the church, was more chore than it was worth. Each face — north, south, east, and west, had to be wound separately. This also meant that they could be set separately, and were, by the man whose job it was to wind the clocks, ring the bells, and generally keep Saint Stephen's ticking over."

I paused here while Barking pursued a regime of facial contortions that suggested that he had something to say in his defence. He finally abandoned the procedure and returned to the analysis of his laces.

"Why did Mister Barking set the clock back?" asked Ivor.

"He didn't," I said. "He set it forward. And he did it simply to support his contention that it was too late to call upon Mister Padget, to acquire the key to the church."

"But, Mister Barking has his own key to the church," pointed out the vicar.

"Of course he does," I said. "He's the verger. This is how he was able to get into the church, change the time on the west-facing clock, and spirit away the tin Hildy."

"The weather vane?" said Ivor. "But it was on top of the church by this time."

"No, it wasn't, was it Mister Barking?"

Barking shook his head slowly.

"Yes it was," said Sally. "We all saw it — it was the tin cow."

"They're both tin, Miss Barnstable. That's Mister Barking's secret. I only realised it when I remembered two seemingly insignificant and unrelated details — the golden tinsel on the steps of the church, and Mister Barking's electroplating enterprise which still has, I believe, some technical issues to work out."

"The cold causes the tin to expand," explained Barking with some resentment aimed, presumably, at the laws of physics. "Then when it contracts again in the sunshine, the brass coating cracks and falls off."

"The municipal budget allocated to Mister Barking for the purchase of bronze with, I think, the clear understanding that he would turn it into cows and heroes, was instead used to finance his industrial innovations," I said. "The bronze Hildy wasn't swapped, it simply shed its golden fleece."

"But, how could we not have noticed?" asked Padget.

"It was dark by then. The moon was behind the clouds. Even Mister Barking only noticed it because he, too, saw the tinsel on the steps before services. To buy time, he hid the original weather vane somewhere in the museum — probably behind the curtain that formed the plinth. Hardly a long term plan, but it served to convince us all that, somehow, the bronze version had been stolen."

"It nearly worked," pointed out Barking, with a disarming, child-like insinuation that this constituted some sort of defence.

"It very nearly did," I agreed. "But then Inspector Wittersham, operating under the advisement of French distillers, committed to searching the museum, and Mister Barking had to act. The clock on the wall of the pub said nine-thirty and when he saw that the clocktower showed only eight-thirty, he set it forward by an hour."

"Wait — the pub clock was also an hour fast? And nobody noticed?" marvelled Ivor.

"It's a pub in dairy country in the middle of winter. The sun goes down at just after four and rises at eight. The only pace that matters is that of the cows, and that's what told me that Miss Barnstable, too, was setting the pub clock ahead by increments, shaving up to an hour off the working day."

"A cow told you?"

"In a manner of speaking. Puckeridge informs me that dairy cattle are very particular about their routine — milking is done by consultation only and according to a strict schedule. And yet, the first time I saw Miss Barnstable leave to milk Hildy, the clock read seven o'clock. The second time, Hildy was mooing a melancholy moan, which Miss Barnstable tried to attribute to a hangover, on the not entirely groundless assumption that a lifetime Londoner wouldn't know that a seven hundred pound cow would be largely immune to such a thing. Hildy was calling out to be milked, but the clock read just after six."

"Miss Barnstable set the clock ahead the first night and third nights?" said Ivor. "Why not the second?"

"Because there was no need, was there Miss Barnstable?"

"You know everything, why don't you explain it to everyone."

"Probably for the best," I agreed. "This is the secret that Miss Barnstable has been keeping. She sets the clock ahead most days for two reasons — it reduces the number of drinks that her father, Soaky Mike, can put away in a day, and it allows her to sneak off early to the forbidden city of Steeple Herding, to spend time with her beloved and betrothed, Constable Kimble."

"Say, where is the constable?" asked Monty.

"Delivering Mister Trimble to the cells," said Ivor. "He'll be back shortly."

"Not immediately," I corrected. "I asked him to look into something for me. In any case, on the second night, Soaky Mike was denied drink, owing to a tragic misunderstanding for which I feel partially responsible. At any rate, the pub was closing early for Saint Stephen's night services. There was no need to set the clock ahead, but not doing so allowed me to take note of the apparent discrepancy in Hildy's routine."

"We all went home, then, without questioning the time," observed Ivor. "All but for Cosmo and Trimble. But why did Trimble want to kill Cosmo? And if he had reason to do so, why didn't he do it sooner?"

"He didn't have cause, sooner," I said. "Cosmo could expose Major Fleming's killer by showing how the seemingly impossible murder was committed."

"It was the footprints in the snow, wasn't it, Anty?" enthused Aunt Azalea. "You're such a clever boy."

"Thank you Aunty, but that's really not that clever. It is, nevertheless, what Cosmo concluded, when I, inspired by the story of Good King Wenceslas, raised the subject."

"But if Mister Millicent was wrong, what cause did Everett have to kill him?" asked Ivor.

"Cosmo was telling everyone who'd listen that he had figured out who killed Flaps Fleming, and that he was saving the unveiling for the final chapter of his book. He also had learned that he didn't need his uncle's permission to write the aforementioned book. It is this that he wished to confide in Everett, and it's this that got him killed." I spoke 'this' with a bit of a topspin and simultaneously withdrew from my breast pocket a copy of *Copyright Infringement and Remedy*.

"Is that Boodle's pamphlet on copyright law?" asked Ivor. "In which he explains that you're safest writing books after your subject has died by causes natural or otherwise?"

"It is," I confirmed. "It's also the single piece of evidence that would hang Everett Trimble."

"How?"

"For that, I would ask that you take another cup of seasonal solvent and bear with me. Feel free to speak amongst yourselves."

We drained the iron cauldron and, contrary to my clear instructions, conversation was, at best, laboured. Finally the doorbell chimed, Puckeridge performed a pirouette followed by a *grande jetée* out the door, and within moments he was back and introducing Constable Kimble and guest.

The effect on the assembly was exactly as expected — half of them gasped as they would had they seen a ghost. The other half, very pointedly, didn't.

Specifically, it was Sally, Barking, and, to a lesser degree, Soaky Mike, who finally managed some variation of "Flaps —

you're alive!" and crowded around the new arrival with such tearful rejoicing that I almost regretted bringing it to an end.

"Anty," said Aunty, taking matters in hand. "That's not Flaps Fleming."

"No, indeed," I agreed. "This is not Flaps Fleming. This is the man who has been posing as Flaps Fleming for the past six months. Ladies and gentlemen, may I present Josilyn Boodle, solicitor."

Boodle smiled sheepishly and waved even more sheepishly. In fact if sheep were ever to take to smiling and waving, they would do well to start by imitating his form.

"Hello," he said.

"Is this true, Mister Boodle?" demanded Ivor.

"Ah, well, only in the purely practical sense, but, yes."

"Only in the practical sense?" said Ivor, slipping into a higher register that I'd heard from him to date. It suited him, strangely. "In what other sense does one impersonate a war hero?"

"The legal sense, mainly. Since I fully paid off my bar bill, it can't be said that I was in any way profiting from my innocent pastime. No harm done, and all that."

"No harm done? We were investigating a murder. You were questioned during the course of that investigation and you chose to say nothing of what I think we all agree was a fairly pertinent detail."

"In retrospect, yes, of course, you're quite right, Inspector," said Boodle. "But you'll recall, you told me that you had identified the killer. You implied quite plainly that the investigation was largely a formality. I saw no need to further, ehm, confuse the issue."

"Whatever led you to suspect that Mister Boodle was impersonating the major?" Ivor asked me.

"Apart from the fact that it was the only possible explanation, you mean?" I replied. "I knew that Aunty Azalea wasn't lying..."

"Thank you, Anty," said Aunty.

"Goes without saying, Aunty. The only other possibility, apart from an actual ghost, was that there were two Flaps Fleming. However, to answer your original question, Inspector, I received the initial inspiration from an inspection of the body combined with a seemingly drunken aspersion cast by Soaky Mike."

"About the major's inability to shift gears with a missing eye?" asked Ivor, incredulously.

"With a missing left eye, to be precise. But the corpse had an eyepatch over the right eye. Possibly because he forgot or because he has poor spatial awareness, Mister Boodle wore his patch over the wrong eye."

"Oh, very well," sighed Ivor. "But why Mister Boodle, specifically?"

"Having concluded that somebody must be impersonating Flaps Fleming, it stood to reason that it must be someone with intimate knowledge of the major's history and habits, but was unknown to everyone in Graze Hill. Mister Boodle was the only possible suspect. He confirmed it himself when he mentioned Cosmo's literary aspirations. The only way Mister Boodle could have known about the book is if it was he who was playing the hero at the Sulky Cow."

"But he looks nothing like him," insisted Aunty.

"Oh, I don't know," I said. "He's tall and thin, and he's

cultivated a military moustache in the style much favoured by the modern flying ace. Add an eyepatch and intimate knowledge of his affairs, and Mister Boodle could easily pass for Flaps Fleming to someone who's never laid eyes on him in his life."

"But, we've all met him," pointed out Padget. "At church, at the pub, at his home..."

"I once had two dear friends — to each other, you understand, I couldn't bear either of them — two dear friends who had a terrible falling out over the soloist in a production of *No, No, Nanette*, which ran for twelve weeks at Drury Lane."

"Please don't, Mister Boisjoly," said Ivor.

"I assure you it's pertinent," I claimed. "Or at the very least a valuable moral lesson for all. These two friends — such close friends, in fact, that I could never remember which we called Giggles and which we called Gander — agreed on everything. The phenomenon was so pronounced, in fact, that it became regular practice to only pose any question to one or the other — they were sure to agree on meat or fish, red or white, or on which horse they would wish to lose their identical pearl collar studs at Sandown."

"I thought you said there was a point," Ivor helpfully reminded me.

"I'm getting to it, although I confess that which I've provided thus far has been largely background material. This is the bit that will start to resonate, I feel — one day Giggles... or possibly Gander, I'm going to have to ask you to grant me some latitude on that... one day Giggles comes into the Juniper, our mutual club, singing a snappy tune and the praises of the musical he saw the night before, *No, No, Nanette*."

"Without Gander?" asked Monty.

"They were friends, Monty, not Siamese twins," I said. "But indeed, Giggles set about correcting that very oversight, and he'd brought a gift of a box seat for his friend, Gander, for that very evening."

"How sweet," opined Aunt Azalea.

"Everyone thought so. Especially Gander. He went, and he, too, naturally, enjoyed the show immensely, except for one key element."

"The soloist," guessed Barking.

"Hated her. Came in the next day doing an amusing impersonation of Nanette that made her sound like a startled carthorse."

"A bit strong," said Monty.

"He insisted that his interpretation of her performance was uncannily accurate. Giggles, naturally, took offence, and words were had. But, these were old and dear friends, and a compromise was found — Gander gifted Giggles a ticket for that night's performance, so that he might take the hard, objective view and, if he would be guided by Gander, lay off the opium until after the show."

"Yes, thank you, Mister Boisjoly, that's very insightful," said Ivor.

"Almost there, Inspector," I alleged. "The next day, Giggles agrees that he had been biassed on first viewing and that Nanette was *not* the finest performance he'd ever seen in London, but the finest performance that anyone had ever seen anywhere, anytime, and that poor Gander must be losing his faculties. It was sad, he said, but he would stand by his old friend, all the way to the sanatorium. Again, an agreement was made, and Gander went that night to Drury Lane to give Nanette one more chance to prove that she wasn't an exceptionally well-trained hyena in circus makeup. The next day, same thing, except that Gander has expanded his imitation of Nanette to include a dance number on locked knees and a curtain-call resembling Swedish callisthenics."

"How did Giggles respond to that?" asked Aunty.

"Less than kindly, I'm afraid," I said. "It came to pass that Giggles had, the previous afternoon, proposed to the lovely Nanette, and she had accepted him."

"Oh, no," lamented Aunty.

"It's always the way. *Best of pals 'til one gets a gal* — a sentiment lifted, ironically enough, from the duet which opens act two of *No, No, Nanette*. Giggles quit the Juniper and settled into the married life. It was fully a year later that the tragic truth came to light — Gander had gone to see a production of *Tip-Toes* at the Haymarket when who should appear in the role of Roberta Van Renssalaer but Nanette. Nostalgic and curious, he meets her at the stage door with a dozen roses and asks after his old friend. Of course, the girl's never heard of any Giggles or whatever his real name is, but she's got a mystery of her own — she always wondered what happened to the girl with whom she used to alternate the title role in *No, No, Nanette* — one night one of them would play Nanette and the other would play Sue, the next night the other way round."

"It was a long, hard road, Mister Boisjoly, but can we agree that we've arrived?" asked Ivor.

"We have," I concluded. "Each of you saw a different Flaps Fleming — at different times and in different places."

"Not I," said the vicar. "I visited the major on numerous occasions in his home, and he regularly attended Sunday services."

"Morning services, Mister Padget," I pointed out.

"Well, yes... Oh, yes. I see what you mean."

"Everyone who saw Mister Boodle's lively interpretation of the role of Major Aaron Fleming at the Sulky Cow did most of their spiritual spadework in the evenings," I said, "while the real Flaps was enjoying evenings in with my maiden aunt. Puckeridge is the only one among us to have met both Flaps Flemings, because he attended morning services. There he saw the major, but obviously made no connection between that retiring stranger and the extroverted hero from the pub."

"But surely someone must have encountered both men in their true identities," speculated Padget.

"And yet, they didn't," I persisted. "Owing to an historic feud, none of you ever visit Steeple Herding, and Mister Boodle spends most of the week in London. Cosmo, Mister Barking, Everett, and Miss Barnstable only ever met the man they thought was Flaps at the Sulky Cow. Mister Padget and Aunty Boisjoly only ever saw their Flaps Fleming at church or in his home, Tannery Lodge, where until very recently he lived the life of a recluse."

"I fear that I still must differ with you, Mister Boisjoly," differed Padget. "Mister Barking visited the major many times in his home, as did Mister Millicent."

"Did you, Mister Barking?" I asked.

"Not as such, no."

"No. And neither did Cosmo. Barking didn't wish it to be known that he was making no progress on the statue of the hero, and Cosmo had similar incentive with regards to his book. Indeed, the fact that they both claimed to have been there and to have seen the missing war memorabilia was what convinced me that neither of them had."

"What war memorabilia?" asked Ivor.

"Exactly. There wasn't any. For reasons which will be made very clear in a moment, Major Fleming eschewed all documentary souvenirs from his time in France." I once again held up my pamphlet on copyright law. "It was only when Cosmo saw this, with a clear picture of the man he knew as Flaps Fleming, that he realised the truth. Unfortunately for Cosmo, even then he managed to get the wrong end of the stick entirely — he thought that he was in a position to blackmail Mister Boodle into assigning him the rights to the life story of Flaps Fleming."

"And this is what he told Everett Trimble," guessed Ivor.

"It is. Until then, Everett could hardly believe his luck — Mister Boodle's innocent appropriation of the fame of Flaps Fleming had lain the blame for his crime firmly on Aunt Azalea, but then Cosmo called him aside — no doubt enthusiastically, the poor ninny — to show him what he'd found."

"It's damning," said Kimble. "But how does it prove that Mister Trimble killed Major Fleming?"

"He's the only one who could have," I explained. "Monty visited the pub on Christmas eve, where he met the regulars. Everett had long harboured resentment about his father's suicide, but it was only when Monty told him that Flaps Fleming had, for his own safety, sent Sargeant Trimble back to England, that he was able to focus his ire. Everett is an impetuous, hot-headed man, with ten years of anger boiling inside him. He left the pub, he went to Tannery Lodge, he met the second Flaps Fleming and he expressed his dissatisfaction with the war effort."

"The tracks in the snow weren't from Tannery Lodge to the pub," twigged Kimble. "They were the other way round."

"Exactly," I confirmed. "And by the time the snow began to fall on Christmas eve, Cosmo, Monty, and Mister Padget were in each other's company, and in a position to alibi Miss Barnstable. Soaky Mike was left alone in the pub, but we know the tracks weren't his, because — sorry Soaky — they were more or less straight."

"But what about the fire? Who stoked it up on Christmas morning?" asked Kimble.

"Nobody did. Everett is impulsive, but he's also a quick thinker. He put a frozen log on the fire — a practice which I note is common even here at Herding House — it defrosts and then finally begins to burn. It would have given the impression that it was placed on the fire hours later. To obscure the evidence of the extra ash, which we all noticed, and perhaps to give us something else to think about, Everett added volume one of the war diaries of Charles à Court Repington."

I pulled over to the soft shoulder, conversationally, and allowed everyone to catch up in their own time. Alice and the kitchen maid were laying a generous sideboard of roast beef and Yorkshire pudding, steamed root vegetables, roast potatoes glazed, I believe, in goose fat, and sherry gravy. To see us through the interim, Puckeridge distributed champagne cocktails.

Ivor happened to be standing next to Monty when they raised their glasses in season's greetings, but then stopped before the champagne could do him any good.

"Hang on, Boisjoly," he said. "What about Monty? He knew the real Flaps Fleming during the war. We saw them in the picture together at Tannery Lodge."

I sipped my cocktail, for theatrical effect, before saying, "Oh, Monty knew that the man he met at the Sulky Cow wasn't Major Fleming, but he didn't expect him to be, did you Monty?"

"No, sir, I did not," said Monty. "I was expecting something else altogether."

"I daresay you were. This, finally, was Monty's secret — he knew that the other man who survived the encounter with the Zeppelins that fateful evening in December, 1917, the man who moved directly to the Fleming country seat of Graze Hill and took up a solitary lifestyle in Tannery Lodge, was no more Major Aaron Fleming than Mister Boodle is. Isn't that correct, Monty?"

"It is. I didn't expect this blighter, though."

"No, you were expecting, I think, Second Lieutenant Carwyn 'Cardiac' Rhys-Thomas, a man who had joined the air force to escape three wives and a mountain of debt. A man who, when he found himself the lone survivor of his entire squadron, with a bandaged face and his pick of new identities, became the wealthy, reclusive hero, Major Flaps Fleming."

"Exactly so," said Monty. "Wasn't bothered by it, you understand, only came by to kid him about it. Didn't expect to get him killed."

"Well, dash it man, why didn't you say anything when he was?" demanded Ivor.

"I think that I can answer that, too," I said.

"Well, of course you can."

"Monty didn't speak up for the same reason that he's allowed Cardiac to live as Flaps Fleming for all these years — he has a second secret. Monty really is the spy of Dunkirk."

CHAPTER TWENTY

The Twist in the Case of the Ghost of Christmas Morning

"A Bosch spy? In Hertfordshire?"

Nobody in particular said those exact words but it was a sentiment broadly shared and expressed. I held up a conciliatory palm.

"Not a Bosch spy," I said. "A double-agent, acting on behalf of His Majesty's intelligence services, to dazzle and confuse the nation's enemies with false information."

"How could you possibly know that?" asked Monty.

"You told me, Monty, when you said that you knew my father, and furthermore had fraternised with him in the VIP mess. Up to but not, notably, including the day he was put out of my mother's misery, my father's signal strength was his capacity for self-preservation. He contrived to see out the war in the offices of military intelligence, in Whitehall, where no mere fighter pilot would ever have made his acquaintance. You met him there when you accepted the daring and, may I say, heroic role of passing disinformation to the enemy under the assumed identity of the spy the Germans had placed in the Dunkirk squadron — the real Montgomery Hern-Fowler."

"Okay, that's it," said Ivor. "You're tight. Is anyone who they claim to be?"

"I think we have a full and frank census now, Inspector."

"Well, if this isn't Flight-Lieutenant Hern-Fowler, who is it?"

"I should have thought that would have been obvious," I said. "This is Major Aaron 'Flaps' Fleming."

"You are tight."

"That's as may be, but the real Montgomery Hern-Fowler is half-German. Spent his formative years skating on the Rhine and scaling the Zugspitze. This Montgomery Hern-Fowler doesn't know the German word for dachshund which, by the way, is dachshund."

"That doesn't make him Major Fleming," argued Ivor.

"No, it doesn't," I conceded. "I confess I'm guessing a bit now, on the strength of that photograph in Tannery Lodge. The man we thought was Flaps Fleming was second from the left, and in the middle was the man we took to be Montgomery Hern-Fowler. It seems much more likely that a posed squadron photograph would place the captain in the centre. However, it also explains why Monty didn't reveal his true identity until he knew that whoever was going about killing Flaps Flemings was fully satisfied that he'd got them all."

"But, where have you been since the war ended?" asked Aunty.

"I'm not at liberty to say, my dear," said Monty. "But

Anty is almost spot-on, but for an important point of posterity — Montgomery Hern-Fowler was half-Jerry, it's true, but he was the double-agent, sending all manner of fairytale to Bosch command. When he died — fighting for England, I'll have you know — I took his place. After the war, there was still work to be done, and it was best done in the name with which I ended the war. I'm retired from all that now, which is why I finally returned to Graze Hill."

"And you wrote to Mister Padget to say that you were coming. He, in his dual roles of local vicar and community blabbermouth, let it slip to Cardiac, which is why he was preparing to up sticks. He broke off his engagement with Aunt Azalea, and he arranged with his solicitor to sign over all his worldly goods, or at any rate those of Major Fleming."

"And that's why he said goodbye that day in the pub," mused Barking, wistfully.

"No, I recognise it's a bit of a trial without a programme, Mister Barking, but that was Josilyn Boodle. You've never met Flaps Fleming."

"Oh, right you are." Barking brooded on this for a scant moment. "Then why did he say goodbye that day in the pub?"

"Because he knew he'd been rumbled, didn't he?" I pointed out. "He'd been told by Cardiac that anyone else who could identify him was dead. But suddenly and without warning Monty appears. Not only did he know the real Flaps Fleming, he recounted that absurd ghost story and obliged Boodle to confirm it."

"Just a bit of fun," said Monty.

"You weren't curious what had happened to Cardiac?"

"Only slightly," said Monty with a shrug. "I knew that

246

Cardiac was using my identity and that worked well for our purposes — if Aaron Fleming was in Hertfordshire he could hardly be working for British Intelligence. I was surprised when this chap turned up but, knowing Cardiac, I reckoned he'd sold the Flaps Fleming cover and moved on."

"You thought he'd franchised your name?"

"Wouldn't put it past him. He was a rogue, a blighted scoundrel with a history that would shame a Frenchman." Monty looked hard into the fire, which reflected and danced in his eyes. "And he was one of the four finest lads I've ever known."

Aunty Azalea slipped her arm into Monty's and tipped her head onto his shoulder, and there was a general warm chumminess as we all looked at something in the fire.

"More champagne, please, Puckeridge," I said. "And pour some out for the staff."

More popping and pouring followed, and I took a position next to the Christmas tree.

"Ladies and gentlemen, I give you Flaps Fleming, hero of the hour."

"I think that's you, Anthony, if I may call you Anthony," said Monty.

"If, as I suspect is the case, we are soon to be related by marriage, you may even call me Anty, if it won't cause awkward moments," I said. "But you are nevertheless the hero of the hour, or you soon will be. Miss Barnstable, I believe there's something for you beneath the tree."

Sally looked at me with the sullen suspicion with which I will always lovingly associate her, and then approached the tree. As advertised, she found an ornate, festive envelope with her name on it. She turned away and opened it, and then turned back to me.

"What's all this then?"

"It's the deed to Constable Kimble's family farm," I said. "When the real Aaron Fleming has signed it, which I feel confident he will do if he wants my blessing for his marriage, full title will fall to you both."

"But, what about the Sulky Cow? I can't leave Soaky alone in the pub."

"Your father will doubtless want to be of service on the farm, what with you converting it into a bijoux residence for Hildy, my favourite cow. If you'll just hand that envelope to Mister Barking..."

Sally took up another gift from beneath the tree. Barking stepped forward, accepted and opened it.

"It's the deed to the Sulky Cow," he said, as though speaking an unfamiliar language.

"What a relief," I said. "I was afraid it might be another commission for a statue, or a shares offer on one of your visionary schemes, for neither of which, Mister Barking, have you any talent. Just as soon as Flaps has settled a reasonable market price on Miss Barnstable and Soaky for the purchase of their pub, you are no longer a blacksmith, sculptor, yo-yo hopeful and comically inept swindler — you're a pub landlord, free to set the prices as you see fit."

"I don't know what to say."

"Then say nothing, Mister Barking. Merry Christmas. It's very much its own reward, I find, spending other people's money. Talking of which, Mister Padget, I believe you'll find under the tree a cheque for a very generous contribution to the Saint Stephen's renovation fund, including a specific endowment for returning the clocktower to its original state, and budgetary surpluses for an organ, heating, a roof, or any other mad extravagance which takes your fancy. Will that satisfy requirements, Miss Barnstable?"

"Me? What have I got to do with it?"

"Ah, now we get to the dark, mysterious secret of the enigmatic Reverend Padget. He longs for you and Constable Kimble to marry at Saint Stephen's, an eventuality which he hopes will bring together the sundered citizens of Graze Hill and Steeple Herding."

"We're getting married in Saint Bartholomew's," announced Kimble, with the sweet, simple certitude of one who has yet to cross a wife's better judgement. Sally crossed her arms and addressed him silently beneath hooded eyes. "I mean, if that's what you want, of course," Kimble added with judicious haste.

"It'll be just like Romeo and Juliet," I said, "without the emotive poetry of a suicide pact — apologies to those who haven't seen it yet. Now, who've we missed? Ah, Inspector Wittersham."

"I'm just happy to have this all settled."

"Good, because that's all you're getting. Finally we have the stolid, solid, Mister Puckeridge, without whose expertise I would almost certainly have struggled with these baffling puzzles for another half day, possibly longer."

"It's a pleasure just to be of service," said Puckeridge from behind a mask of perfect composure.

"Then you'll be pleased to know that this is what the

future has in store for you," I said. "When the real Flaps Fleming has made an honest woman of my aunt and resumed his role at the centre of municipal affairs, this house will be positively shaking to the foundations with nibs and nobility."

"Oh, yes?" Puckeridge glanced at the former Monty.

"Here and there, I suppose, once in a bit," said Authentic Flaps. "The occasional Prime Minister, from time to time, can't really be avoided, in my position. Edward, obviously..."

"*Prince* Edward, sir?"

"For the moment."

Puckeridge, finally, smiled openly, and swallowed his champagne in a single throw.

The morning of December 28, 1928 was cold and crisp and clear. Hertfordshire rolled away past the window of our compartment in gleaming, glorious blue and white. I was to miss the spellbinding charm of dairy country until a village derby of weddings planned for Spring, and until then I would reflect on my newly enlarged and rediscovered family, on Hildy the Graze Hill Golden, and on the terrible sacrifice of brave lads who died for me and my country and each other.

Vickers, who must always sit in the direction of travel or he forgets he's on a train and is susceptible to anxiety when he looks out the window, was leafing through volume two of Charles à Court Repington's war diary. At some point, perhaps ten minutes out of Steeple Herding, he raised his eyes and then followed my gaze out the window and to the skies. I had been watching Graze Hill, which was now a gentle, bucolic, white and evergreen rise on the horizon.

Above it, a heretofore unseen puff of cottony mist had formed, seemingly from nothing. Possibly it was an escaped bit of errant steam from the locomotive. But then, from within the cloud, sprung four biplanes — Sopwith Camels, I expect — flying in smooth, solid formation. They were war artefacts, clearly, and they bore battle wounds of torn fabric, bullet holes, and burns. The planes kept pace with the train for a few moments, and then banked, somehow upward, toward the heavens, and were gone.

Vickers and I shared the sort of look that two adults might exchange after having seen, say, a leprechaun. Vickers nodded, subtly, and returned to his book, and I to my musings on the mysteries and marvels of this world and the next.

Anty Boisjoly Mysteries

I hope that you enjoyed *The Case of the Ghost of Christmas Morning* and I hope that you had at least a little difficulty figuring out how and who dunnit, and above all that you enjoyed the journey. Obviously I hope that you'll recommend Anty Boisjoly to your friends and even any enemies that you think might one day come round to your way of thinking.

While you're at it, you might tell them as well that there's an entire series of Anty Boisjoly mysteries:

The Case of the Canterfell Codicil
The first Anty Boisjoly mystery
In *The Case of the Canterfell Codicil*, Wodehousian gadabout and clubman Anty Boisjoly takes on his first case when his old Oxford chum and coxswain is facing the gallows, accused of the murder of his wealthy uncle. Not one but two locked-room mysteries later, Boisjoly's pitting his wits and witticisms against a subversive butler, a senile footman, a single-minded detective-inspector, an irascible goat, and the eccentric conventions of the pastoral Sussex countryside to untangle a multi-layered mystery of secret bequests, ancient writs, love triangles, revenge, and a teasing twist in the final paragraph.

The Case of the Ghost of Christmas Morning

The one you just read

In *The Case of the Ghost of Christmas Morning*, clubman, *flaneur*, idler and sleuth Anty Boisjoly pits his sardonic wits against another pair of impossible murders. This time, Anty Boisjoly's Aunty Boisjoly is the only possible suspect when a murder victim stands his old friends a farewell drink at the local, hours after being murdered.

The Tale of the Tenpenny Tontine

The dual duel dilemma

It's another mystifying, manor house murder for bon-vivant and problem-solver Anty Boisjoly, when his clubmate asks him to determine who died first after a duel is fought in a locked room. The untold riches of the Tenpenny Tontine are in the balance, but the stakes only get higher when Anty determines that, duel or not, this was a case of murder.

The Case of the Carnaby Castle Curse

The scary one (Anty Boisjoly number four — due in early 2022)

The ancient curse of Carnaby Castle has begun taking victims again — either that, or someone's very cleverly done away with the new young bride of the philandering family patriarch, and the chief suspect is none other than Carnaby, London's finest club steward.

Anty Boisjoly's wits and witticisms are tested to their frozen limit as he sifts the superstitions, suspicions, and age-old schisms of the medieval Peak District village of Hoy to sort out how it was done before the curse can claim Carnaby himself.

Made in the USA
Monee, IL
11 June 2022

97642015R00144